The Moonlit Veil

Fairy tales, Folk tales, Legends & Mythology, Volume 5

Patrick William Lee

Published by Starlit Tales Publishing, 2024.

THE MOONLIT VEIL

First edition. September 2, 2024.

Copyright © 2024 Patrick William Lee.

ISBN: 979-8227504739

Written by Patrick William Lee.

Table of Contents

To those who believe in the magic of stories,

To the dreamers who see beyond the ordinary,

And to the brave souls who dare to protect the delicate balance
between worlds.

May this tale remind you that even in the darkest of nights,

A single light can guide the way.

For Elara, and for all who walk the path of courage and love.

Chapter 1: The Whispering Forest

In the heart of the world, untouched by the encroaching hands of time and civilization, there lay an ancient forest that had stood for countless millennia. The Whispering Forest, as it was known to those who lived on its fringes, was a place of wonder and mystery, a place where the natural world seemed to hold its breath, where the very air buzzed with secrets too ancient and profound for mortal minds to comprehend. The trees here were not just trees; they were guardians of the old ways, their twisted trunks and gnarled branches reaching skyward as though in supplication to the heavens.

The villagers who lived in the shadow of this great forest spoke of it in hushed tones, their voices dropping to whispers as they recounted the legends passed down from their ancestors. The Whispering Forest was alive, they said—not just with the usual cacophony of birdsong and rustling leaves, but with something far older, something that moved in the spaces between shadows, where the light of the sun could not reach.

It was said that the forest had a voice of its own, a voice that could only be heard by those who listened with their hearts rather than their ears. To the uninitiated, the soft susurrations that echoed through the trees might have sounded like nothing more than the wind weaving its way through the leaves. But to those who understood, to those who had grown up with the stories of the forest, the whispers were messages, fragments of a language as old as the world itself.

The stories told of the Night Spirits—ethereal beings that emerged only under the light of the full moon, their forms shifting and shimmering like mist over a still pond. These spirits were neither malevolent nor benevolent; they simply were, as much a part of the natural order as the rising of the sun or the changing of the seasons. The villagers spoke of them with a mixture of awe and fear, for while the spirits had never harmed anyone, their presence was a reminder of the thin line that separated the world of the living from that of the dead.

At the center of these tales was the legend of the Moonlit Veil, a mysterious phenomenon that occurred only once every few years, when the moon was at its fullest and the night was clear and still. On such nights, it was said, a shimmering, translucent barrier would appear deep within the forest, separating the world of the living from the realm of the spirits. The veil was both beautiful and terrible, a thing of light and shadow that seemed to pulse with its own inner life.

For as long as anyone could remember, the villagers had been warned never to venture into the forest on the night of the full moon. To do so was to risk crossing the veil, to risk stepping into a world from which there might be no return. But the legend of the Moonlit Veil was more than just a cautionary tale; it was a story of connection, of the invisible threads that bound the living and the dead, the past and the present, the seen and the unseen.

The village of Elmsworth, nestled at the edge of the Whispering Forest, had always been a quiet place, its people content to live simple lives in harmony with the land. The villagers were farmers and craftsmen, hunters and healers, their days filled with the rhythms of nature, the cycles of planting and harvest, birth and death. Life here moved at its own pace, unhurried and untroubled by the outside world.

But there was one among them who was different, one who had never been content with the simple life of the village, who had always felt the pull of the forest, the lure of the unknown. Her name was Elara, a girl of sixteen summers, with hair the color of autumn leaves and eyes that seemed to hold all the secrets of the world. Elara had been born on the night of a full moon, and from the moment she had drawn her first breath, it was clear that she was special.

The villagers had always been wary of Elara, for she was unlike any child they had ever known. Even as a baby, she had been quiet and watchful, her gaze following the movements of the trees and the play of light and shadow with an intensity that was almost unsettling. As she grew older, this strange connection to the forest only deepened. Elara could often be found wandering among the trees, her footsteps light and sure, as though she knew the forest like the back of her hand.

It was not just her affinity for the forest that set Elara apart; it was also the way the forest seemed to respond to her. The villagers would often speak in whispers of how the trees seemed to bend towards her, their leaves rustling in a language only she could understand, how animals that would normally flee at the sight of a human would approach her without fear. Some said she had been touched by the spirits, that she was a child of the forest itself.

Elara's parents, though proud of their daughter, were also afraid for her. They had heard the stories, had seen the way the other villagers looked at her, and they knew that Elara was different in a way that could not be easily explained. They tried to keep her close, to shelter her from the forest that seemed to call to her, but Elara was like the wind—free and untamed, impossible to hold onto.

As Elara grew older, her fascination with the Whispering Forest and the legend of the Moonlit Veil only deepened. She would spend hours listening to the stories of the elders, asking questions that no one could answer, searching for clues in the ancient texts that had been passed down through the generations. She longed to see the Moonlit Veil for herself, to witness the Night Spirits in all their otherworldly glory. But more than that, she wanted to understand—understand why she felt such a deep connection to the forest, why the spirits seemed to call to her in her dreams.

The villagers, though wary of Elara's curiosity, could not help but be drawn to her as well. There was something about her that was both captivating and unsettling, a sense of power and mystery that seemed to hover around her like a shadow. Children would follow her into the forest, hoping to catch a glimpse of the magic she seemed to carry with her, while the elders would watch her from a distance, their eyes filled with a mixture of fear and reverence.

It was on a cool autumn evening, as the village prepared for the coming of the full moon, that Elara's journey truly began. The day had been unusually warm for the season, the sky a brilliant blue that seemed to stretch on forever. As the sun dipped below the horizon, the air grew crisp, and a thin mist began to rise from the forest floor, curling around the trees like ghostly fingers.

Elara stood at the edge of the forest, her heart pounding with anticipation. She had been planning this night for weeks, waiting for the perfect moment to slip away from the village and venture deep into the forest, where the Moonlit Veil was said to appear. She knew it was dangerous, knew that the villagers would be furious if they found out, but the pull of the forest was too strong to resist.

She had packed a small bag with supplies—bread and cheese, a flask of water, a knife for protection—and had told her parents she was going to bed early. They had been relieved, thinking that perhaps Elara was finally starting to listen to their warnings, finally beginning to understand the dangers of the forest. But Elara had no intention of staying in bed. As soon as the village had fallen silent, she had slipped out of the house and made her way to the edge of the forest.

The moon was just beginning to rise, a sliver of silver in the darkening sky, its light casting long shadows on the ground. Elara took a deep breath, feeling the cool air fill her lungs, and stepped into the forest.

The trees closed in around her, their branches intertwining overhead to form a dense canopy that blocked out the sky. The only light came from the moon, which filtered through the leaves in thin, silvery beams, casting eerie patterns on the forest floor. The air was filled with the sounds of the night—crickets chirping, the rustle of leaves in the breeze, the distant hoot of an owl. But underneath it all, Elara could hear something else, something that made the hairs on the back of her neck stand on end.

The whispers.

They were faint at first, almost indistinguishable from the rustling of the leaves, but as Elara ventured deeper into the forest, they grew louder, more distinct. It was as though the trees were speaking to one another, passing secrets from one to the next, secrets that had been buried in the earth for centuries. The language was foreign, unlike anything Elara had ever heard before, but there was something familiar about it, something that tugged at the edges of her memory.

Elara walked on, her steps sure and steady, her senses alert. The path she was following was one she had traveled many times before, but tonight it felt different, as though the forest itself was alive, watching her, guiding her. The whispers grew louder, more insistent, and Elara found herself straining to catch the words, to understand what they were saying.

The moon had risen higher now, its light spilling through the trees and casting the forest in an otherworldly glow. Elara felt a shiver run down her spine as she continued to walk, the air growing colder with each step. She knew she was getting close. The Moonlit Veil was said to appear in a clearing deep within the forest, a place where the trees parted to reveal a patch of sky that was always clear, no matter the weather.

As she walked, Elara's thoughts turned to the stories she had heard as a child, the tales of the Night Spirits that had filled her with both wonder and fear. The spirits were said to be as old as the forest itself, beings of pure energy that had once roamed the earth freely, before they had been bound to the forest by a powerful enchantment. The Moonlit Veil was their prison, a barrier that kept them separated from the mortal world, but also protected them from the dangers that lay beyond.

The spirits were not like the ghosts that haunted the stories of other villages; they were not the restless souls of the dead, nor were they malevolent beings bent on causing harm. They were something else entirely, something that defied explanation. Some said they were the spirits of the forest itself, the embodiment of its ancient wisdom and power. Others believed they were the remnants of a long-forgotten civilization, beings who had once lived in harmony with nature but had been cursed for their hubris.

Whatever the truth, the Night Spirits had become a part of the village's lore, their presence woven into the very fabric of life in Elmsworth. The villagers respected the spirits, but they also feared them, for they knew that the line between the living and the dead was thin, and that the spirits walked that line with ease.

Elara had always been fascinated by the spirits, had always felt a strange kinship with them. As a child, she had often dreamed of them, had seen their forms flickering in the shadows of the trees, heard their voices whispering in her ear. She had never been afraid, even when the other children spoke of the spirits with dread. To Elara, they were not something to be feared, but something to be understood.

As she walked deeper into the forest, Elara's thoughts were interrupted by a sudden change in the air. The whispers that had been growing louder now fell silent, and the forest around her seemed to hold its breath. The trees, which had been swaying gently in the breeze, now stood still, their branches motionless. The air was thick with anticipation, as though the forest itself was waiting for something to happen.

Elara's heart quickened as she realized that she had reached the clearing. She could see the edge of the trees up ahead, the darkness giving way to a patch of open sky. The moon, now fully risen, bathed the clearing in its silvery light, illuminating the ground in a way that made the grass and flowers seem to glow.

She stepped into the clearing, her breath catching in her throat as she took in the sight before her. The Moonlit Veil was there, just as the legends had described it—a shimmering, translucent barrier that seemed to hover in the air, separating the clearing from the dense forest beyond. The veil was like nothing Elara had ever seen, its surface rippling like water, catching the light of the moon and refracting it into a thousand different colors.

For a moment, Elara could only stand there, awestruck by the beauty of it. The veil was mesmerizing, its surface shifting and changing with every passing second, as though it was alive. She could see the Night Spirits moving behind it, their forms barely visible, like shadows in a dream. They moved with a grace that was both ethereal and unsettling, their bodies flickering in and out of existence, never fully solid, never fully real.

Elara took a step closer, her heart pounding in her chest. She could feel the pull of the veil, a magnetic force that seemed to draw her in, calling to her with a voice that was both familiar and foreign. The whispers were back, but this time they were coming from the veil itself, a chorus of voices that echoed in her mind, urging her to come closer, to reach out and touch the veil.

She hesitated, her hand hovering in the air just inches from the surface of the veil. The legends had warned of the dangers of crossing the veil, of the thin line that separated the living from the dead. But Elara couldn't shake the feeling that she was meant to be here, that the veil was calling to her for a reason.

Taking a deep breath, she reached out and touched the veil.

The moment her fingers brushed the surface, the world around her seemed to shift. The air grew colder, the light of the moon dimming as though a cloud had passed over it. The whispers grew louder, more urgent, filling her mind with a cacophony of voices that she couldn't understand.

Elara's heart raced as she felt the veil give way beneath her fingers, its surface parting like water to allow her hand to pass through. A wave of cold air rushed out, chilling her to the bone, but she didn't pull back. She could feel the presence of the Night Spirits on the other side, their energy crackling in the air like static electricity.

She took another step forward, her hand now fully submerged in the veil. The whispers were all around her, a constant hum that vibrated through her body, making her feel as though she was standing on the edge of something vast and unknowable. She could see the spirits more clearly now, their forms shifting and changing as they moved closer to the veil, as though drawn to her presence.

For a moment, Elara was tempted to step through the veil, to cross the boundary that separated her world from theirs. But something held her back, a small voice in the back of her mind that reminded her of the warnings, of the dangers that lay beyond the veil.

Reluctantly, she pulled her hand back, feeling the veil close around her fingers as she stepped away. The whispers faded, the spirits retreating into the shadows as the forest around her seemed to exhale, releasing the breath it had been holding.

Elara stood there for a long time, her mind racing with what she had just experienced. She knew she had been close, so close to crossing the veil, to stepping into a world that no mortal had ever seen. But she also knew that the veil was not something to be taken lightly, that its power was far greater than anything she could comprehend.

As she turned to leave the clearing, she couldn't shake the feeling that she had been changed by the experience, that the veil had left its mark on her in some way. The forest around her seemed different now, the trees taller, the shadows darker. The whispers were still there, but they were softer now, more subdued, as though the forest was watching her, waiting to see what she would do next.

Elara made her way back to the village, her thoughts a whirlwind of questions and doubts. She knew she couldn't keep what she had seen a secret, that the villagers would have to be told. But she also knew that they wouldn't understand, that they would see her encounter with the veil as a dangerous flirtation with forces beyond their control.

As she reached the edge of the forest, the village lights twinkling in the distance, Elara made a decision. She would return to the forest, she would seek out the Moonlit Veil again. But this time, she would be prepared. This time, she would find the answers she was looking for.

And as she stepped out of the forest and into the light of the village, she knew that her journey had only just begun.

Chapter 2: The Enchanted Village

The village of Elmsworth had stood for centuries, nestled comfortably at the edge of the Whispering Forest, a place both revered and feared by those who called it home. The village was secluded, far from the bustle of the larger towns and cities that dotted the landscape, and its people had learned to live in harmony with the natural world that surrounded them. Life in Elmsworth was simple, unhurried, and deeply rooted in traditions that had been passed down through the generations, just like the legend of the Moonlit Veil.

Elmsworth was not just a village; it was a living, breathing entity, shaped by the land and the forest that cradled it. The houses, made of timber and stone, seemed to grow organically from the earth, their roofs covered in thick thatch that blended seamlessly with the surrounding foliage. The streets were narrow and winding, more like pathways than roads, lined with wildflowers and shaded by the ancient oaks that stood as silent sentinels at the village's borders.

The people of Elmsworth were a close-knit community, bound together by shared histories, beliefs, and a deep respect for the land that sustained them. They were farmers, shepherds, and artisans, their days filled with the rhythms of planting and harvest, the birth of new life and the turning of the seasons. The village had a timeless quality to it, as though it existed outside the flow of the rest of the world, untouched by the changes that had swept across the land.

At the center of the village was a large square, where the villagers would gather for markets, festivals, and other communal events. The square was dominated by an ancient oak tree, its massive trunk and sprawling branches a testament to the passage of time. The oak was said to be as old as the village itself, its roots intertwined with those of the Whispering Forest. It was here, beneath the shade of this great tree, that the villagers would come together to share stories, sing songs, and pass down the legends that had been woven into the fabric of their lives.

One such legend, and perhaps the most revered of all, was the story of the Moonlit Veil. The tale had been told and retold countless times, each generation adding its own details and embellishments, but the essence of the story remained the same. The Moonlit Veil was a mystical barrier that appeared deep within the Whispering Forest on the night of the full moon. It was said to separate the world of the living from the realm of the Night Spirits, ethereal beings who were neither dead nor alive, but something in between.

The Night Spirits were a mystery, their origins lost to time. Some believed they were the spirits of the forest itself, the guardians of the ancient trees and the creatures that dwelled within them. Others thought they were the remnants of a forgotten civilization, beings who had once lived in harmony with nature but had been cursed for their hubris. Whatever the truth, the spirits were a part of the village's lore, and their presence was both revered and feared.

The villagers spoke of the Moonlit Veil with a mixture of awe and caution, for while it was a thing of beauty, it was also a reminder of the thin line that separated their world from the unknown. To cross the veil was to step into a realm from which one might never return, and so the villagers took care to avoid the forest on the night of the full moon, when the veil was said to be at its most powerful.

But not everyone in Elmsworth shared this fear. There was one among them who had always been fascinated by the legend of the Moonlit Veil, a young girl named Elara.

Elara had been born sixteen years earlier, on a night much like this one, when the moon hung full and heavy in the sky, casting its silver light over the village and the forest beyond. From the moment she had drawn her first breath, it was clear that she was different. Even as a baby, Elara had been quiet and watchful, her large, amber eyes taking in the world around her with a curiosity that was almost unsettling. As she grew, this curiosity only deepened, and it became apparent that Elara had a connection to the forest that went beyond mere fascination.

Unlike the other children of the village, who preferred to play in the safety of the square or the fields, Elara was drawn to the Whispering Forest. She would often wander among the trees, her small feet treading lightly on the forest floor, her eyes wide with wonder as she explored the hidden paths and secret glades that only she seemed able to find. The forest seemed to welcome her, its trees bending their branches toward her as if in greeting, the animals watching her with eyes that were almost human in their understanding.

The villagers noticed this, of course, and while they were proud of Elara's bravery, they were also wary. The forest was a place of power, a place where the veil between worlds was thin, and they feared what might happen if Elara strayed too far. Her parents, in particular, were concerned, for they had heard the stories, had seen the way the other villagers looked at their daughter, and they knew that Elara was different in a way that could not be easily explained.

But no matter how much they tried to keep her close, to discourage her from wandering into the forest, Elara could not be dissuaded. The pull of the forest was too strong, the allure of the unknown too great. She was like the wind—free and untamed, impossible to hold onto. And so, they allowed her to explore, hoping that in time she would grow out of this strange obsession, that she would come to understand the dangers of the forest and the importance of staying close to the village.

But as Elara grew older, her fascination with the forest only deepened. She became obsessed with the stories of the Night Spirits and the Moonlit Veil, spending hours listening to the elders recount the legends, asking questions that no one could answer, searching for clues in the ancient texts that had been passed down through the generations. She would sit for hours beneath the old oak tree in the village square, her gaze fixed on the distant line of the forest, her mind filled with visions of the spirits and the veil that separated their world from hers.

The villagers, though wary of Elara's curiosity, could not help but be drawn to her as well. There was something about her that was both captivating and unsettling, a sense of power and mystery that seemed to hover around her like a shadow. Children would follow her into the forest, hoping to catch a glimpse of the magic she seemed to carry with her, while the elders would watch her from a distance, their eyes filled with a mixture of fear and reverence.

It was on a cool autumn evening, as the village prepared for the coming of the full moon, that Elara's journey truly began.

The day had been unusually warm for the season, the sky a brilliant blue that seemed to stretch on forever. As the sun dipped below the horizon, the air grew crisp, and a thin mist began to rise from the forest floor, curling around the trees like ghostly fingers. The villagers, mindful of the stories of the Moonlit Veil, hurried to finish their tasks and return to the safety of their homes before the moon rose.

But Elara was not among them. She stood at the edge of the forest, her heart pounding with anticipation, her thoughts consumed by the stories she had heard as a child, the tales of the Night Spirits that had filled her with both wonder and fear. She knew that the Moonlit Veil was said to appear tonight, deep within the forest, and she was determined to see it for herself.

She had been planning this night for weeks, waiting for the perfect moment to slip away from the village and venture deep into the forest. She knew it was dangerous, knew that the villagers would be furious if they found out, but the pull of the forest was too strong to resist.

The moon was just beginning to rise, a sliver of silver in the darkening sky, its light casting long shadows on the ground. Elara took a deep breath, feeling the cool air fill her lungs, and stepped into the forest.

The trees closed in around her, their branches intertwining overhead to form a dense canopy that blocked out the sky. The only light came from the moon, which filtered through the leaves in thin, silvery beams, casting eerie patterns on the forest floor. The air was filled with the sounds of the night—crickets chirping, the rustle of leaves in the breeze, the distant hoot of an owl. But underneath it all, Elara could hear something else, something that made the hairs on the back of her neck stand on end.

The whispers.

They were faint at first, almost indistinguishable from the rustling of the leaves, but as Elara ventured deeper into the forest, they grew louder, more distinct. It was as though the trees were speaking to one another, passing secrets from one to the next, secrets that had been buried in the earth for centuries. The language was foreign, unlike anything Elara had ever heard before, but there was something familiar about it, something that tugged at the edges of her memory.

Elara walked on, her steps sure and steady, her senses alert. The path she was following was one she had traveled many times before, but tonight it felt different, as though the forest itself was alive, watching her, guiding her. The whispers grew louder, more insistent, and Elara found herself straining to catch the words, to understand what they were saying.

The moon had risen higher now, its light spilling through the trees and casting the forest in an otherworldly glow. Elara felt a shiver run down her spine as she continued to walk, the air growing colder with each step.

She knew she was getting close. The Moonlit Veil was said to appear in a clearing deep within the forest, a place where the trees parted to reveal a patch of sky that was always clear, no matter the weather.

As she walked, Elara's thoughts turned to the stories she had heard as a child, the tales of the Night Spirits that had filled her with both wonder and fear. The spirits were said to be as old as the forest itself, beings of pure energy that had once roamed the earth freely, before they had been bound to the forest by a powerful enchantment. The Moonlit Veil was their prison, a barrier that kept them separated from the mortal world, but also protected them from the dangers that lay beyond.

The spirits were not like the ghosts that haunted the stories of other villages; they were not the restless souls of the dead, nor were they malevolent beings bent on causing harm. They were something else entirely, something that defied explanation. Some said they were the spirits of the forest itself, the embodiment of its ancient wisdom and power. Others believed they were the remnants of a long-forgotten civilization, beings who had once lived in harmony with nature but had been cursed for their hubris.

Whatever the truth, the Night Spirits had become a part of the village's lore, their presence woven into the very fabric of life in Elmsworth. The villagers respected the spirits, but they also feared them, for they knew that the line between the living and the dead was thin, and that the spirits walked that line with ease.

Elara had always been fascinated by the spirits, had always felt a strange kinship with them. As a child, she had often dreamed of them, had seen their forms flickering in the shadows of the trees, heard their voices whispering in her ear. She had never been afraid, even when the other children spoke of the spirits with dread. To Elara, they were not something to be feared, but something to be understood.

As she walked deeper into the forest, Elara's thoughts were interrupted by a sudden change in the air. The whispers that had been growing louder now fell silent, and the forest around her seemed to hold its breath. The trees, which had been swaying gently in the breeze, now stood still, their branches motionless. The air was thick with anticipation, as though the forest itself was waiting for something to happen.

Elara's heart quickened as she realized that she had reached the clearing. She could see the edge of the trees up ahead, the darkness giving way to a patch of open sky. The moon, now fully risen, bathed the clearing in its silvery light, illuminating the ground in a way that made the grass and flowers seem to glow.

She stepped into the clearing, her breath catching in her throat as she took in the sight before her. The Moonlit Veil was there, just as the legends had described it—a shimmering, translucent barrier that seemed to hover in the air, separating the clearing from the dense forest beyond. The veil was like nothing Elara had ever seen, its surface rippling like water, catching the light of the moon and refracting it into a thousand different colors.

For a moment, Elara could only stand there, awestruck by the beauty of it. The veil was mesmerizing, its surface shifting and changing with every passing second, as though it was alive. She could see the Night Spirits moving behind it, their forms barely visible, like shadows in a dream. They moved with a grace that was both ethereal and unsettling, their bodies flickering in and out of existence, never fully solid, never fully real.

Elara took a step closer, her heart pounding in her chest. She could feel the pull of the veil, a magnetic force that seemed to draw her in, calling to her with a voice that was both familiar and foreign. The whispers were back, but this time they were coming from the veil itself, a chorus of voices that echoed in her mind, urging her to come closer, to reach out and touch the veil.

She hesitated, her hand hovering in the air just inches from the surface of the veil. The legends had warned of the dangers of crossing the veil, of the thin line that separated the living from the dead. But Elara couldn't shake the feeling that she was meant to be here, that the veil was calling to her for a reason.

Taking a deep breath, she reached out and touched the veil.

The moment her fingers brushed the surface, the world around her seemed to shift. The air grew colder, the light of the moon dimming as though a cloud had passed over it. The whispers grew louder, more urgent, filling her mind with a cacophony of voices that she couldn't understand.

Elara's heart raced as she felt the veil give way beneath her fingers, its surface parting like water to allow her hand to pass through. A wave of cold air rushed out, chilling her to the bone, but she didn't pull back. She could feel the presence of the Night Spirits on the other side, their energy crackling in the air like static electricity.

She took another step forward, her hand now fully submerged in the veil. The whispers were all around her, a constant hum that vibrated through her body, making her feel as though she was standing on the edge of something vast and unknowable. She could see the spirits more clearly now, their forms shifting and changing as they moved closer to the veil, as though drawn to her presence.

For a moment, Elara was tempted to step through the veil, to cross the boundary that separated her world from theirs. But something held her back, a small voice in the back of her mind that reminded her of the warnings, of the dangers that lay beyond the veil.

Reluctantly, she pulled her hand back, feeling the veil close around her fingers as she stepped away. The whispers faded, the spirits retreating into the shadows as the forest around her seemed to exhale, releasing the breath it had been holding.

Elara stood there for a long time, her mind racing with what she had just experienced. She knew she had been close, so close to crossing the veil, to stepping into a world that no mortal had ever seen. But she also knew that the veil was not something to be taken lightly, that its power was far greater than anything she could comprehend.

As she turned to leave the clearing, she couldn't shake the feeling that she had been changed by the experience, that the veil had left its mark on her in some way. The forest around her seemed different now, the trees taller, the shadows darker. The whispers were still there, but they were softer now, more subdued, as though the forest was watching her, waiting to see what she would do next.

Elara made her way back to the village, her thoughts a whirlwind of questions and doubts. She knew she couldn't keep what she had seen a secret, that the villagers would have to be told. But she also knew that they wouldn't understand, that they would see her encounter with the veil as a dangerous flirtation with forces beyond their control.

As she reached the edge of the forest, the village lights twinkling in the distance, Elara made a decision. She would return to the forest, she would seek out the Moonlit Veil again. But this time, she would be prepared. This time, she would find the answers she was looking for.

And as she stepped out of the forest and into the light of the village, she knew that her journey had only just begun.

Chapter 3: The Night of the Full Moon

The full moon had always held a special place in the life of Elmsworth, casting its silvery light over the village and the Whispering Forest, bathing the world in an ethereal glow that seemed to blur the line between reality and fantasy. The villagers had a deep respect for the full moon, for it was on such nights that the legend of the Moonlit Veil became more than just a story—it became a living, breathing part of their world.

The day had been one of anticipation, a quiet tension settling over Elmsworth as the sun began its descent, leaving the sky awash with hues of pink and orange. The villagers went about their daily tasks with a sense of urgency, knowing that they had to finish before the sun dipped below the horizon and the full moon rose to take its place in the sky. The fields were cleared, the animals brought into their pens, and the last of the autumn crops harvested and stored away.

The village square, usually bustling with activity, was unusually quiet as the evening approached. The market stalls had been packed up early, the usual chatter and laughter replaced by the murmur of hushed conversations. The villagers exchanged worried glances, their thoughts turning to the stories of the Night Spirits and the Moonlit Veil. Even the children, who usually played until the last light of day, were subdued, staying close to their parents as the shadows lengthened.

Elara, however, was not among them. She had spent the day in restless preparation, her thoughts consumed by the legend of the Moonlit Veil and the strange experience she had had in the forest the night before. She had not told anyone about what she had seen, not even her parents, for she knew they would only worry and try to stop her from going back into the forest. But Elara was determined. She could not ignore the pull of the forest, the whispers that had haunted her dreams for as long as she could remember.

As the sun began to set, Elara stood at the edge of the forest, her heart pounding with anticipation. She had packed a small satchel with supplies—a flask of water, a piece of bread, and the knife she had used the night before. She knew the path she would take, the same path that had led her to the clearing and the Moonlit Veil. But this time, she would go further, she would find the answers she was looking for.

The first sliver of the full moon appeared on the horizon, its light casting long shadows on the ground. Elara took a deep breath, feeling the cool air fill her lungs, and stepped into the forest.

The trees closed in around her, their branches intertwining overhead to form a dense canopy that blocked out the last of the daylight. The only light came from the moon, which filtered through the leaves in thin, silvery beams, casting eerie patterns on the forest floor. The air was filled with the sounds of the night—crickets chirping, the rustle of leaves in the breeze, the distant hoot of an owl. But underneath it all, Elara could hear something else, something that made the hairs on the back of her neck stand on end.

The whispers.

They were faint at first, almost indistinguishable from the rustling of the leaves, but as Elara ventured deeper into the forest, they grew louder, more distinct. It was as though the trees were speaking to one another, passing secrets from one to the next, secrets that had been buried in the earth for centuries. The language was foreign, unlike anything Elara had ever heard before, but there was something familiar about it, something that tugged at the edges of her memory.

Elara walked on, her steps sure and steady, her senses alert. The path she was following was one she had traveled many times before, but tonight it felt different, as though the forest itself was alive, watching her, guiding her. The whispers grew louder, more insistent, and Elara found herself straining to catch the words, to understand what they were saying.

The moon had risen higher now, its light spilling through the trees and casting the forest in an otherworldly glow. Elara felt a shiver run down her spine as she continued to walk, the air growing colder with each step. She knew she was getting close. The Moonlit Veil was said to appear in a clearing deep within the forest, a place where the trees parted to reveal a patch of sky that was always clear, no matter the weather.

As she walked, Elara's thoughts turned to the stories she had heard as a child, the tales of the Night Spirits that had filled her with both wonder and fear. The spirits were said to be as old as the forest itself, beings of pure energy that had once roamed the earth freely, before they had been bound to the forest by a powerful enchantment. The Moonlit Veil was their prison, a barrier that kept them separated from the mortal world, but also protected them from the dangers that lay beyond.

The spirits were not like the ghosts that haunted the stories of other villages; they were not the restless souls of the dead, nor were they malevolent beings bent on causing harm. They were something else entirely, something that defied explanation. Some said they were the spirits of the forest itself, the embodiment of its ancient wisdom and power. Others believed they were the remnants of a long-forgotten civilization, beings who had once lived in harmony with nature but had been cursed for their hubris.

Whatever the truth, the Night Spirits had become a part of the village's lore, their presence woven into the very fabric of life in Elmsworth. The villagers respected the spirits, but they also feared them, for they knew that the line between the living and the dead was thin, and that the spirits walked that line with ease.

Elara had always been fascinated by the spirits, had always felt a strange kinship with them. As a child, she had often dreamed of them, had seen their forms flickering in the shadows of the trees, heard their voices whispering in her ear. She had never been afraid, even when the other children spoke of the spirits with dread. To Elara, they were not something to be feared, but something to be understood.

As she walked deeper into the forest, Elara's thoughts were interrupted by a sudden change in the air. The whispers that had been growing louder now fell silent, and the forest around her seemed to hold its breath. The trees, which had been swaying gently in the breeze, now stood still, their branches motionless. The air was thick with anticipation, as though the forest itself was waiting for something to happen.

Elara's heart quickened as she realized that she had reached the clearing. She could see the edge of the trees up ahead, the darkness giving way to a patch of open sky. The moon, now fully risen, bathed the clearing in its silvery light, illuminating the ground in a way that made the grass and flowers seem to glow.

She stepped into the clearing, her breath catching in her throat as she took in the sight before her. The Moonlit Veil was there, just as the legends had described it—a shimmering, translucent barrier that seemed to hover in the air, separating the clearing from the dense forest beyond. The veil was like nothing Elara had ever seen, its surface rippling like water, catching the light of the moon and refracting it into a thousand different colors.

For a moment, Elara could only stand there, awestruck by the beauty of it. The veil was mesmerizing, its surface shifting and changing with every passing second, as though it was alive. She could see the Night Spirits moving behind it, their forms barely visible, like shadows in a dream. They moved with a grace that was both ethereal and unsettling, their bodies flickering in and out of existence, never fully solid, never fully real.

Elara took a step closer, her heart pounding in her chest. She could feel the pull of the veil, a magnetic force that seemed to draw her in, calling to her with a voice that was both familiar and foreign. The whispers were back, but this time they were coming from the veil itself, a chorus of voices that echoed in her mind, urging her to come closer, to reach out and touch the veil.

She hesitated, her hand hovering in the air just inches from the surface of the veil. The legends had warned of the dangers of crossing the veil, of the thin line that separated the living from the dead. But Elara couldn't shake the feeling that she was meant to be here, that the veil was calling to her for a reason.

Taking a deep breath, she reached out and touched the veil.

The moment her fingers brushed the surface, the world around her seemed to shift. The air grew colder, the light of the moon dimming as though a cloud had passed over it. The whispers grew louder, more urgent, filling her mind with a cacophony of voices that she couldn't understand.

Elara's heart raced as she felt the veil give way beneath her fingers, its surface parting like water to allow her hand to pass through. A wave of cold air rushed out, chilling her to the bone, but she didn't pull back. She could feel the presence of the Night Spirits on the other side, their energy crackling in the air like static electricity.

She took another step forward, her hand now fully submerged in the veil. The whispers were all around her, a constant hum that vibrated through her body, making her feel as though she was standing on the edge of something vast and unknowable. She could see the spirits more clearly now, their forms shifting and changing as they moved closer to the veil, as though drawn to her presence.

For a moment, Elara was tempted to step through the veil, to cross the boundary that separated her world from theirs. But something held her back, a small voice in the back of her mind that reminded her of the warnings, of the dangers that lay beyond the veil.

Reluctantly, she pulled her hand back, feeling the veil close around her fingers as she stepped away. The whispers faded, the spirits retreating into the shadows as the forest around her seemed to exhale, releasing the breath it had been holding.

Elara stood there for a long time, her mind racing with what she had just experienced. She knew she had been close, so close to crossing the veil, to stepping into a world that no mortal had ever seen. But she also knew that the veil was not something to be taken lightly, that its power was far greater than anything she could comprehend.

As she turned to leave the clearing, she couldn't shake the feeling that she had been changed by the experience, that the veil had left its mark on her in some way. The forest around her seemed different now, the trees taller, the shadows darker. The whispers were still there, but they were softer now, more subdued, as though the forest was watching her, waiting to see what she would do next.

Elara made her way back to the village, her thoughts a whirlwind of questions and doubts. She knew she couldn't keep what she had seen a secret, that the villagers would have to be told. But she also knew that they wouldn't understand, that they would see her encounter with the veil as a dangerous flirtation with forces beyond their control.

As she reached the edge of the forest, the village lights twinkling in the distance, Elara made a decision. She would return to the forest, she would seek out the Moonlit Veil again. But this time, she would be prepared. This time, she would find the answers she was looking for.

And as she stepped out of the forest and into the light of the village, she knew that her journey had only just begun.

Chapter 4: The Veil Unveiled

The Whispering Forest had always been a place of mystery, its ancient trees towering over the village of Elmsworth, casting long shadows over the land. But for Elara, the forest was more than just a collection of trees; it was a living, breathing entity, a place where the line between reality and legend blurred. And tonight, as the moon climbed higher in the sky, casting its silver light over the world, Elara felt the forest calling to her, urging her deeper into its embrace.

It had been several nights since she last ventured into the forest, since she had felt the pull of the Moonlit Veil and the whispers of the Night Spirits. She had tried to push the experience from her mind, to focus on the mundane tasks of daily life, but the memory of that night had lingered, haunting her dreams and filling her thoughts with a restless energy that she could not shake.

And so, as the full moon rose once again, Elara found herself standing at the edge of the forest, her heart pounding with anticipation. She had made up her mind—tonight, she would go deeper into the forest than she ever had before. She would find the hidden glade where the Moonlit Veil appeared, and she would uncover the truth behind the legends that had captivated her for so long.

The village was quiet, the only sound the soft rustle of leaves in the breeze. Elara knew that the villagers were safely tucked away in their homes, wary of the full moon and the stories that came with it. But Elara was not afraid. She was determined to find the truth, no matter the cost.

She took a deep breath, feeling the cool night air fill her lungs, and stepped into the forest. The trees closed in around her, their branches intertwining overhead to form a dense canopy that blocked out the light of the moon. The air was thick with the scent of earth and moss, and the sounds of the night—crickets chirping, the rustle of leaves, the distant hoot of an owl—filled the air.

Elara moved quickly, her steps sure and steady as she followed the path she had traveled many times before. But tonight, the path felt different, as though the forest itself was guiding her, urging her onward. The whispers that had haunted her dreams were back, faint at first, almost indistinguishable from the rustling of the leaves, but growing louder with each step she took.

The moon had risen higher now, its light filtering through the leaves in thin, silvery beams, casting eerie patterns on the forest floor. Elara felt a shiver run down her spine as she continued to walk, the air growing colder with each step. She knew she was getting close.

The path began to narrow, the trees closing in around her, their branches forming a tunnel that seemed to stretch on forever. Elara's heart quickened as she pushed forward, her breath coming in short, shallow gasps. The whispers were louder now, a constant hum that vibrated through her body, filling her mind with a sense of urgency.

Finally, the tunnel of trees opened up into a small clearing, bathed in the light of the full moon. Elara stepped into the clearing, her breath catching in her throat as she took in the sight before her.

The Moonlit Veil was there, just as the legends had described it—a shimmering, translucent barrier that seemed to hover in the air, separating the clearing from the dense forest beyond. The veil was like nothing Elara had ever seen, its surface rippling like water, catching the light of the moon and refracting it into a thousand different colors.

For a moment, Elara could only stand there, awestruck by the beauty of it. The veil was mesmerizing, its surface shifting and changing with every passing second, as though it was alive. She could see the Night Spirits moving behind it, their forms barely visible, like shadows in a dream. They moved with a grace that was both ethereal and unsettling, their bodies flickering in and out of existence, never fully solid, never fully real.

Elara took a step closer, her heart pounding in her chest. She could feel the pull of the veil, a magnetic force that seemed to draw her in, calling to her with a voice that was both familiar and foreign. The whispers were back, but this time they were coming from the veil itself, a chorus of voices that echoed in her mind, urging her to come closer, to reach out and touch the veil.

She hesitated, her hand hovering in the air just inches from the surface of the veil. The legends had warned of the dangers of crossing the veil, of the thin line that separated the living from the dead. But Elara couldn't shake the feeling that she was meant to be here, that the veil was calling to her for a reason.

Taking a deep breath, she reached out and touched the veil.

The moment her fingers brushed the surface, the world around her seemed to shift. The air grew colder, the light of the moon dimming as though a cloud had passed over it. The whispers grew louder, more urgent, filling her mind with a cacophony of voices that she couldn't understand.

Elara's heart raced as she felt the veil give way beneath her fingers, its surface parting like water to allow her hand to pass through. A wave of cold air rushed out, chilling her to the bone, but she didn't pull back. She could feel the presence of the Night Spirits on the other side, their energy crackling in the air like static electricity.

She took another step forward, her hand now fully submerged in the veil. The whispers were all around her, a constant hum that vibrated through her body, making her feel as though she was standing on the edge of something vast and unknowable. She could see the spirits more clearly now, their forms shifting and changing as they moved closer to the veil, as though drawn to her presence.

For a moment, Elara was tempted to step through the veil, to cross the boundary that separated her world from theirs. But something held her back, a small voice in the back of her mind that reminded her of the warnings, of the dangers that lay beyond the veil.

Reluctantly, she pulled her hand back, feeling the veil close around her fingers as she stepped away. The whispers faded, the spirits retreating into the shadows as the forest around her seemed to exhale, releasing the breath it had been holding.

Elara stood there for a long time, her mind racing with what she had just experienced. She knew she had been close, so close to crossing the veil, to stepping into a world that no mortal had ever seen. But she also knew that the veil was not something to be taken lightly, that its power was far greater than anything she could comprehend.

As she stood there, staring at the veil, Elara couldn't shake the feeling that the veil was more than just a barrier. It was a gateway, a portal to another realm, a place where the rules of the mortal world did not apply. The Night Spirits were not just shadows; they were beings of immense power, beings who existed in a world that was both beautiful and terrifying.

Elara took a deep breath, her mind racing with questions. What lay beyond the veil? What was the true nature of the Night Spirits? And why had the veil called to her, drawn her to this place?

As she pondered these questions, the whispers began to fade, the spirits retreating into the shadows as the light of the moon began to wane. Elara knew that it was time to leave, that she had pushed the boundaries of the veil as far as she could. But as she turned to leave the clearing, she couldn't shake the feeling that her journey was far from over.

The path back to the village was a blur, Elara's mind consumed by the experience she had just had. She moved quickly, her steps light and sure, her senses heightened by the energy that still crackled in the air around her.

As she reached the edge of the forest, the village lights twinkling in the distance, Elara made a decision. She would return to the forest, she would seek out the Moonlit Veil again. But this time, she would be prepared. This time, she would find the answers she was looking for.

And as she stepped out of the forest and into the light of the village, she knew that her journey had only just begun.

Chapter 5: The Guardian of the Veil

The Whispering Forest had a way of enveloping those who entered it in an embrace of both wonder and trepidation. For as long as she could remember, Elara had felt this duality—the allure of its mysteries and the silent warning that lay hidden in its depths. Each night she ventured into the forest, the call of the Moonlit Veil grew stronger, pulling her deeper into its ancient heart. But tonight was different. Tonight, the air was thick with a sense of impending revelation, a feeling that something profound awaited her.

Elara had scarcely slept since her last encounter with the Moonlit Veil. The sight of the shimmering barrier, the glimpse of the Night Spirits dancing gracefully behind it, had ignited within her a burning desire to understand the true nature of the veil and its connection to the world she knew. The whispers that had haunted her since childhood were louder now, filling her mind with fragments of an ancient language she could almost grasp. She had a sense that the veil held answers to questions she hadn't yet learned to ask.

As the full moon rose high in the sky, casting its pale light over the world, Elara knew that she could no longer resist its pull. She left her home in silence, careful not to wake her parents, who had long since given up trying to understand her fascination with the forest. They feared for her safety, but Elara could not be swayed. The forest was a part of her, and the veil was calling her once more.

The village was quiet as she made her way to the edge of the forest, the only sound the soft rustling of leaves in the breeze. The trees seemed to part for her as she entered, their branches reaching out like welcoming arms. The path was familiar now, etched into her memory from countless nights of wandering, but tonight it felt different. The forest was alive with energy, the air crackling with a tension that set her nerves on edge.

The deeper she went, the louder the whispers became. They swirled around her, a chorus of voices that seemed to be speaking directly to her soul. She could feel their urgency, their need to be heard, and she quickened her pace, drawn ever closer to the source of the whispers—the Moonlit Veil.

When she reached the clearing, the veil was already there, its surface rippling like water under the light of the moon. The Night Spirits moved gracefully behind it, their forms shifting and changing as they danced in and out of existence. But tonight, Elara's attention was not on the spirits or the veil itself. Her eyes were drawn to something else—someone else.

Standing at the edge of the veil was a figure, tall and shrouded in shadows, their form barely distinguishable from the darkness of the forest. The figure was clad in a cloak of deep midnight blue, its fabric shimmering as though woven from the very essence of the night. A hood obscured their face, leaving only a pair of eyes visible—eyes that gleamed with an otherworldly light.

Elara's heart skipped a beat, a mixture of fear and curiosity washing over her. She had never seen another person in the forest at night, much less one who seemed so intimately connected to the veil. The figure's presence was both unsettling and strangely comforting, as though they were a part of the forest itself, an embodiment of the mysteries it held.

For a long moment, neither of them moved. Elara stood frozen at the edge of the clearing, her breath caught in her throat, while the figure remained still, their gaze fixed on the veil. Then, slowly, the figure turned to face her, and Elara felt a jolt of recognition deep within her. This was no ordinary person; this was the Guardian of the Veil.

"Elara," the figure spoke, their voice a soft, melodious whisper that seemed to resonate with the very air around them. "You have come."

The sound of her name on the guardian's lips sent a shiver down Elara's spine. How did they know her name? And what did they mean by saying she had come, as if they had been expecting her?

"Yes," Elara replied, her voice trembling slightly. "I had to. The veil... it called to me."

The guardian nodded, their gaze unwavering. "It is as I feared. The veil has sensed your presence, your curiosity, and it has responded. But you must understand, Elara—the veil is not just a doorway, not just a barrier. It is a sacred boundary, one that must never be crossed."

Elara took a step forward, her eyes wide with a mixture of fear and determination. "But why? What lies beyond the veil? What are the Night Spirits, and why are they here?"

The guardian sighed, their eyes softening with something akin to pity. "You are brave, Elara, but your bravery may lead you down a path of great danger. The veil is not just a boundary between the mortal world and the realm of the spirits. It is a protection, for both worlds. The Night Spirits are beings of immense power, beings who once roamed freely between worlds. But their power is too great, too volatile. To protect both realms, a veil was woven between them, a veil that keeps the spirits bound to their own realm."

Elara's heart raced as the guardian's words sank in. "But why can't they be free? If they're not malevolent, why must they be imprisoned?"

"It is not a matter of malevolence," the guardian replied, their voice tinged with sorrow. "It is a matter of balance. The Night Spirits are beings of pure energy, beings who exist beyond the physical constraints of our world. Their presence here, in the mortal realm, would disrupt the natural order. The veil was created to maintain that balance, to ensure that the realms remain separate and intact."

Elara frowned, her mind racing with questions. "But why am I drawn to the veil? Why do the whispers call to me?"

The guardian was silent for a moment, as if considering how much to reveal. Finally, they spoke, their voice low and serious. "Elara, you are different from the others in your village. You have always felt a connection to the forest, to the veil, because you are not entirely of this world."

Elara's breath caught in her throat. "What do you mean?"

The guardian took a step closer, their gaze piercing. "There is a part of you, Elara, that is tied to the realm beyond the veil. It is why the veil calls to you, why you can hear the whispers of the Night Spirits. You are a bridge between worlds, a being who can exist in both realms. But that is also why your presence here is so dangerous."

"Dangerous?" Elara whispered, her voice barely audible.

"Yes," the guardian replied, their tone grave. "Your presence has already begun to disrupt the balance. The veil is weakening, responding to your connection to the other realm. If you were to cross the veil, to enter the realm of the spirits, it could unravel the very fabric of both worlds."

Elara felt a cold wave of fear wash over her. She had never imagined that her curiosity, her desire to understand the veil, could have such dire consequences. "What should I do?" she asked, her voice trembling. "How can I make it right?"

The guardian was silent for a moment, their gaze distant as if searching for an answer. "You must leave the forest, Elara. You must return to your village and live as the others do, away from the veil. The connection you feel to the other realm will never fully fade, but with time, the veil will strengthen, and the balance will be restored."

Elara's heart sank at the thought of leaving the forest, of abandoning the quest for answers that had consumed her for so long. "But what about the Night Spirits? What about the veil?"

"The spirits will remain as they are, bound to their realm, and the veil will continue to protect both worlds," the guardian said gently. "But you must resist the urge to return, Elara. The temptation will be great, but you must not give in. If you do, the consequences could be catastrophic."

Elara felt a lump form in her throat. "And what about you? Will you always be here, guarding the veil?"

The guardian nodded slowly. "It is my duty, and it has been so for many lifetimes. I am bound to the veil, just as the spirits are bound to their realm. I will remain here as long as the veil stands."

Tears welled up in Elara's eyes. She had come so far, had uncovered so much, only to be told that she must walk away from it all. "I don't want to leave," she whispered, her voice breaking. "I don't want to forget."

The guardian stepped closer, their expression softening with compassion. "You will not forget, Elara. The memories of this place, of the veil, will stay with you. But you must live your life in the mortal realm, where you belong. It is the only way to protect both worlds."

Elara nodded, tears streaming down her cheeks. She knew the guardian was right, knew that she had no choice but to leave the forest and the veil behind. But it didn't make the decision any easier.

The guardian reached out and gently placed a hand on Elara's shoulder. "You are stronger than you know, Elara. You have the power to protect the veil by staying away, by living your life in the village. Trust in that strength, and know that you are doing what is best for both worlds."

Elara wiped away her tears and looked up at the guardian, determination filling her heart. "I will do as you ask," she said firmly. "

I will leave the forest and live my life in the village. But I won't forget what I've learned here."

The guardian nodded, their gaze filled with a mix of sorrow and pride. "That is all I can ask of you, Elara. Go now, and may the balance be restored."

With one last look at the Moonlit Veil, Elara turned and made her way out of the clearing. The forest was silent as she walked, the whispers of the Night Spirits fading into the distance. But as she reached the edge of the forest and stepped into the light of the village, she couldn't shake the feeling that her journey was far from over.

The days that followed were some of the hardest of Elara's life. She kept her promise to the guardian, staying away from the forest and focusing on her life in the village. But the pull of the veil was always there, a constant hum in the back of her mind, a reminder of the world she had left behind.

She threw herself into her daily tasks, helping her parents with the farm, spending time with friends, and trying to live as the other villagers did. But no matter how hard she tried, she couldn't fully escape the call of the forest. The whispers would come to her in her dreams, the memory of the Night Spirits haunting her thoughts.

Her parents noticed the change in her, the way she seemed distant and distracted, but they didn't press her for answers. They were just glad that she had finally stopped her nightly excursions into the forest, that she was staying close to home where they could keep an eye on her.

But Elara knew that she couldn't keep living like this, torn between two worlds. She had made a promise to the guardian, and she intended to keep it. But she also knew that she couldn't ignore the call of the veil forever.

One night, as the full moon rose high in the sky, Elara made a decision. She would return to the forest one last time, not to cross the veil or disrupt the balance, but to say goodbye to the world that had captivated her for so long.

She left her home in silence, careful not to wake her parents, and made her way to the edge of the forest. The trees seemed to welcome her as she entered, their branches reaching out like old friends. The path was familiar now, etched into her memory from countless nights of wandering, but tonight it felt different. The forest was alive with energy, the air crackling with a tension that set her nerves on edge.

When she reached the clearing, the veil was already there, its surface rippling like water under the light of the moon. The Night Spirits moved gracefully behind it, their forms shifting and changing as they danced in and out of existence. But tonight, Elara's attention was not on the spirits or the veil itself. Her eyes were drawn to something else—the guardian.

The figure stood at the edge of the veil, just as they had before, their form barely distinguishable from the shadows of the forest. But this time, Elara felt no fear, only a deep sense of sadness.

"I came to say goodbye," she said softly, stepping into the clearing.

The guardian turned to face her, their eyes gleaming with an otherworldly light. "I knew you would come," they replied. "The veil has been calling to you."

Elara nodded, her heart heavy. "I don't want to leave, but I know I must."

The guardian's gaze softened. "You have done well, Elara. You have protected the veil by staying away, by living your life in the mortal realm. But I know the pull of the veil is strong, and that you have struggled."

Elara looked down, her voice trembling. "I don't know if I can keep doing this, living in two worlds."

The guardian stepped closer, their voice gentle. "You are stronger than you know, Elara. The connection you feel to the veil will never fully fade, but with time, it will become a part of you, something that you carry with you but do not let consume you."

Elara nodded, tears streaming down her cheeks. "I will try," she whispered.

The guardian reached out and gently placed a hand on Elara's shoulder. "You have a great destiny, Elara, one that is tied to both realms. But that destiny will only be fulfilled if you live your life in the mortal world. Trust in your strength, and know that you are doing what is best for both worlds."

Elara looked up at the guardian, determination filling her heart. "I will do as you ask," she said firmly. "I will live my life in the village and protect the veil by staying away."

The guardian nodded, their gaze filled with a mix of sorrow and pride. "That is all I can ask of you, Elara. Go now, and may the balance be restored."

With one last look at the Moonlit Veil, Elara turned and made her way out of the clearing. The forest was silent as she walked, the whispers of the

Night Spirits fading into the distance. But as she reached the edge of the forest and stepped into the light of the village, she couldn't shake the feeling that her journey was far from over.

Over the following weeks, Elara began to find peace with her decision. She threw herself into village life, forging deeper connections with her family and friends, and finding new purpose in the tasks that had once seemed mundane. The whispers in her dreams grew softer, no longer a constant pull but a gentle reminder of the world beyond the veil.

She would often stand at the edge of the forest, looking out into the shadows and feeling the connection that would always be a part of her. But she did not step into the trees, did not venture into the depths where the veil waited. She had made a promise, and she intended to keep it.

The villagers noticed the change in Elara, how she seemed more present, more grounded. They no longer spoke of her strange connection to the forest with fear, but with a sense of respect, as if they recognized that she held a secret knowledge that set her apart.

As the months passed, Elara found a new sense of purpose. She began to share the stories of the Moonlit Veil and the Night Spirits with the younger children, passing down the legends with a wisdom that came from her own experiences. She became a storyteller, a keeper of the village's lore, and in doing so, she found a way to honor her connection to the veil without crossing the boundary that had been set.

But deep down, Elara knew that the day would come when she would have to face the veil again, when the pull would become too strong to resist. She did not know when that day would come, but she felt a quiet certainty that her journey was not yet complete.

For now, she was content to live her life in the village, to find peace in the balance she had created. But in the quiet moments, when the moon was full and the forest whispered her name, Elara would close her eyes and remember the guardian's words: "You have a great destiny, Elara, one that is tied to both realms."

And she would wait, knowing that when the time came, she would be ready.

Chapter 6: The Forbidden Knowledge

The days that followed Elara's encounter with the Guardian of the Veil were filled with a profound sense of inner turmoil. She had returned to the village with a promise on her lips and a resolve to live in the mortal world, but the whispers of the forest lingered in her mind, tugging at the edges of her consciousness. The Guardian's warning echoed in her thoughts, yet so did the allure of the Moonlit Veil and the mysteries it concealed.

Elara tried to immerse herself in the rhythm of village life, throwing herself into the work of the fields, the tending of animals, and the simple joys of daily existence. She took comfort in the company of her family and friends, in the laughter shared over meals and the warmth of the hearth at night. Yet, beneath the surface, a relentless curiosity gnawed at her, an insatiable need to understand the true nature of the veil and the Night Spirits.

The Guardian had told her to leave the veil alone, to live her life away from its influence, but Elara found herself unable to heed this advice completely. The connection she felt to the veil was not something she could simply sever, no matter how hard she tried. It was as if the veil had become a part of her, woven into the very fabric of her being.

As the days turned into weeks, Elara's resolve began to waver. She could not ignore the feeling that there was something more to the veil, something that the Guardian had not told her. The secrets it held were too tantalizing to resist, and despite the warnings, Elara knew that she had to uncover the truth.

Her thoughts turned to the village elder, a woman named Lysandra, who was said to possess knowledge that few others dared to seek. Lysandra was a figure of both reverence and fear in Elmsworth, a keeper of ancient lore and forgotten truths. She lived on the outskirts of the village, in a small, weathered cottage surrounded by a garden of herbs and flowers. The villagers often sought her counsel on matters of health and healing, but it was whispered that Lysandra knew far more than just the secrets of herbs. She was said to be a seer, a woman who could glimpse the future and commune with the spirits of the forest.

Elara had always been fascinated by Lysandra, though she had never had a reason to visit her. But now, with the Guardian's warnings weighing heavily on her mind and the pull of the veil growing stronger by the day, Elara knew that she needed answers. She needed to understand the true nature of the veil and the Night Spirits, and she believed that Lysandra might hold the key.

One crisp autumn morning, Elara made her way to Lysandra's cottage, her heart pounding with a mixture of excitement and trepidation. The path to the elder's home was lined with trees whose leaves had turned shades of gold and crimson, and the air was filled with the scent of woodsmoke and earth. As Elara walked, she rehearsed in her mind what she would say, how she would explain her need for knowledge without revealing too much of what she had already learned.

When she reached the cottage, Elara hesitated at the gate, her hand hovering over the latch. The garden beyond was wild and untamed, a riot of colors and scents that seemed to pulse with life. Lysandra herself was nowhere to be seen, but Elara could feel her presence, as though the elder was watching her from the shadows.

Taking a deep breath, Elara pushed open the gate and stepped into the garden. The path wound through clusters of herbs and flowers, leading to the cottage door, which stood slightly ajar. Elara approached the door and raised her hand to knock, but before she could, a voice called out from within.

"Come in, child."

Elara started at the sound of Lysandra's voice, which was soft but commanding, carrying with it the weight of years and wisdom. She pushed the door open and stepped inside.

The interior of the cottage was warm and dimly lit, the air thick with the scent of drying herbs and the faint tang of incense. Shelves lined the walls, filled with jars of potions, dried plants, and ancient books. A fire crackled in the hearth, casting flickering shadows across the room.

Lysandra sat in a high-backed chair near the fire, her sharp, gray eyes fixed on Elara as she entered. The elder was a woman of indeterminate age, her silver hair pulled back in a loose braid, her face lined with the marks of time. She wore a simple gown of deep green, and around her neck hung a pendant shaped like a crescent moon, its surface polished to a mirror-like sheen.

Elara felt a surge of nervousness as Lysandra's gaze met hers, but she forced herself to remain calm. She stepped closer to the fire, feeling its warmth on her skin, and met Lysandra's eyes.

"You've come seeking answers," Lysandra said, her voice steady and measured. "But I must warn you, Elara, that the knowledge you seek is not without its dangers. The veil and the spirits it conceals are not things to be trifled with."

Elara nodded, her voice trembling slightly as she spoke. "I know, Lysandra. But I can't ignore the pull of the veil. I need to understand what it is, what it means. Please, if you know anything that can help me, I need to hear it."

Lysandra studied her for a long moment, her eyes searching Elara's face as if weighing her resolve. Finally, she nodded and gestured to a wooden stool beside the fire.

"Sit, child. What you ask is not a simple matter, and the answers you seek may not be what you wish to hear."

Elara sat down, her hands clasped tightly in her lap. She watched as Lysandra reached for a small pouch that hung from her belt and drew out a handful of dried leaves, which she sprinkled into a brass bowl on the table beside her. The leaves began to smolder, filling the air with a sweet, pungent scent that made Elara's head swim.

"Long before our village was founded," Lysandra began, her voice low and rhythmic, "this land was home to a people who lived in harmony with the forest and the spirits that dwelled within it. They were a wise and peaceful people, skilled in the arts of magic and healing, and they held the forest in great reverence, for they knew that it was a place where the veil between worlds was thin."

Elara listened intently, her breath catching in her throat as Lysandra's words painted a picture of a world long past.

"These people understood that the veil was a boundary, a barrier that kept the realms of the living and the spirits separate. But they also knew that the veil was not impenetrable. There were times, particularly during the full moon, when the veil would thin, allowing the spirits to cross into the mortal realm."

Lysandra paused, her eyes narrowing as she continued. "The people of that time were careful to honor the veil and the spirits, to maintain the balance between the realms. But there were some who sought to breach the veil, to wield the power of the spirits for their own gain. These individuals were driven by greed and ambition, blinded to the consequences of their actions."

"What happened to them?" Elara asked, her voice barely above a whisper.

Lysandra's gaze darkened. "They succeeded in breaching the veil, but the power they unleashed was beyond their control. The spirits, freed from their realm, brought chaos and destruction to the mortal world. The balance was shattered, and both realms were plunged into darkness."

Elara shuddered at the thought, imagining the devastation that must have followed. "How was the balance restored?"

"The elders of that time, those who had not been swayed by the promise of power, worked together to weave a new veil, one that was stronger and more resilient. They bound the spirits to their own realm, sealing the breach and restoring the balance. But the cost was great. The veil required constant vigilance, and the elders knew that it could never be breached again."

Lysandra's eyes locked onto Elara's, her gaze intense. "That is why the veil is sacred, why it must never be crossed. The Guardian you encountered is one of the last of those ancient elders, bound to the veil for eternity, charged with protecting it from those who would seek to breach it again."

Elara felt a chill run down her spine as she listened to Lysandra's words. The Guardian's warnings now carried even more weight, and the enormity of what she had discovered settled heavily on her shoulders. But there was still one question that burned in her mind, one that she needed to have answered.

"Lysandra," she began hesitantly, "do you know of any prophecy connected to the veil? The Guardian mentioned something about me being different, about my connection to the veil. Is there something I should know?"

Lysandra's expression softened, and for a moment, Elara thought she saw a flicker of sadness in the elder's eyes. "There is indeed a prophecy, Elara, one that has been passed down through the generations. It is said that in a time of great change, a mortal will be born who possesses the power to breach the veil, to change the fate of both worlds forever."

Elara's heart skipped a beat. "And you think that person is me?"

Lysandra sighed, her gaze shifting to the fire. "I do not know, Elara. The prophecy is vague, its meaning open to interpretation. But there are signs, and you possess certain... qualities that suggest you may be the one foretold."

Elara's mind raced as she tried to process this revelation. "But if I breach the veil, won't it bring the same chaos and destruction as before?"

"That depends on how you approach it," Lysandra replied, her voice measured. "The prophecy speaks of both great danger and great potential. It is said that the one who breaches the veil will either restore the balance or shatter it completely. The outcome is not predetermined; it will be shaped by the choices you make."

Elara felt a weight settle in her chest as the implications of Lysandra's words sank in. She had always known she was different, had always felt a connection to the veil, but she had never imagined that her actions could have such far-reaching consequences.

"What should I do?" she asked, her voice trembling with uncertainty. "How can I know what the right choice is?"

Lysandra reached out and took Elara's hand, her touch warm and reassuring. "You must trust in yourself, Elara. You are stronger than you know, and your heart is pure. The veil may call to you, but it is your choices that will determine the path you take. You must find the balance within yourself before you can restore the balance between the realms."

Elara nodded, her mind still reeling from everything she had learned. The prophecy, the history of the veil, the role she might play in shaping the future—it was almost too much to take in. But she knew that she couldn't turn back now. The knowledge she had gained was both a burden and a gift, and she was determined to use it wisely.

"Thank you, Lysandra," she said, her voice filled with gratitude. "I don't know what the future holds, but I promise I'll do my best to protect the veil and the balance between the realms."

Lysandra smiled, her eyes filled with a warmth that Elara hadn't seen before. "I have faith in you, Elara. The path ahead will be difficult, but I believe you have the strength to walk it."

With that, Lysandra released Elara's hand and stood, moving to a nearby shelf where she retrieved a small, intricately carved wooden box. She returned to Elara's side and placed the box in her hands.

"Take this," Lysandra said. "Inside is a talisman, crafted by the elders long ago. It will help guide you on your journey and protect you from the darker forces that may seek to influence you. Use it wisely."

Elara opened the box and gazed at the talisman within. It was a small, circular pendant made of polished stone, etched with ancient symbols that seemed to pulse with a faint inner light. She felt a sense of calm wash over her as she held it, as though the talisman were a source of strength and clarity.

"Thank you," Elara said, her voice filled with emotion. "I will cherish it."

Lysandra nodded, her expression serious. "Remember, Elara, the veil is more than just a boundary—it is a living entity, one that responds to the energy and intentions of those who seek to interact with it. Your connection to the veil is strong, but it is also fragile. You must tread carefully and be mindful of the balance."

Elara nodded, the weight of Lysandra's words settling heavily in her heart. She stood, slipping the talisman around her neck and tucking it beneath her tunic, where it rested against her skin. The warmth of the stone was a comforting presence, a reminder of the guidance and protection it offered.

As Elara prepared to leave, Lysandra reached out and placed a hand on her shoulder, her gaze filled with a mix of pride and concern.

"Go with caution, Elara," Lysandra said softly. "And remember that you are not alone. The spirits of the forest are watching over you, and you have the strength within you to face whatever lies ahead."

Elara nodded, feeling a surge of gratitude for the elder's wisdom and support. "Thank you, Lysandra. I'll remember your words."

With that, Elara turned and left the cottage, stepping out into the cool autumn air. The sun was beginning to set, casting long shadows across the landscape as she made her way back to the village. The path ahead was uncertain, and the weight of the prophecy hung heavily on her shoulders, but Elara felt a renewed sense of purpose.

She would not shy away from the challenges that lay ahead. She would seek out the truth, uncover the secrets of the veil, and fulfill her destiny—whatever that might be. And she would do so with the knowledge that she was not alone, that she had the strength within her to protect the balance between the realms.

As the village came into view, Elara's thoughts turned to the future. The choices she made in the coming days would shape not only her own fate but the fate of both the mortal world and the realm of the spirits. It was a daunting responsibility, but Elara knew that she could not turn back now.

The veil still called to her, its whispers a constant presence in her mind, but now she understood the gravity of what lay beyond it. The Guardian's warnings and Lysandra's wisdom had opened her eyes to the true nature of the veil and the forces it protected. And with the talisman around her neck, Elara felt a sense of calm and clarity that had eluded her before.

She would return to the forest, seek out the veil, and learn its secrets. But this time, she would do so with caution and respect, mindful of the balance that must be maintained. She would honor the prophecy and her connection to the veil, but she would not allow herself to be consumed by it.

As the first stars began to twinkle in the darkening sky, Elara reached the edge of the village and paused, looking back at the forest that had become such an integral part of her life. The path ahead was shrouded in uncertainty, but Elara felt a sense of resolve deep within her. She would find the answers she sought, and she would do so with the knowledge that she was not alone.

With a deep breath, Elara turned and made her way back into the village, ready to face whatever challenges the future might hold.

Chapter 7: The Lost Song of the Spirits

Elara had always known that the Whispering Forest was full of secrets, but never had she imagined that it could hold the key to understanding the Night Spirits. The revelation from Lysandra about the prophecy had set Elara on a path she could no longer turn away from. She now carried not only the knowledge of her unique connection to the veil but also the heavy burden of what that meant for both worlds. Each day, the whispers grew louder, and with them, an urgency that Elara could not ignore.

The talisman that Lysandra had given her rested against her chest, a constant reminder of the power she carried within her. But it wasn't enough to simply possess the talisman; she needed to understand it, to unlock the secrets it held. She needed to learn the language of the spirits, the ancient tongue that had been lost to time but was still echoed in the whispers that surrounded her.

One morning, as she sat alone in the clearing just outside the village, the first tendrils of autumn mist curling around her, Elara heard the whispers more clearly than ever before. They swirled around her, soft and melodic, almost as if they were trying to tell her something. She closed her eyes, focusing all her attention on the sounds, and that's when she heard it—a melody, faint but unmistakable, woven into the fabric of the whispers.

It was unlike any music Elara had ever heard. It was haunting and beautiful, a song that seemed to resonate with the very soul of the forest. The melody lingered on the edge of her consciousness, elusive and tantalizing, as if it were inviting her to follow it, to seek out its source.

Elara's heart raced as she opened her eyes, the melody still echoing in her mind. Could this be the song that Lysandra had hinted at—the song of the Night Spirits, the key to understanding their language? If so, it was more than just a song; it was a bridge, a way to communicate with the spirits and learn the truth about the veil and the realms beyond it.

But as Elara focused on the melody, she realized something troubling. The song was incomplete. There were gaps in the melody, missing notes that left the tune fragmented and unfinished. It was as if the song had been broken into pieces, scattered across the forest, waiting to be found.

Elara knew then what she had to do. She had to find the missing pieces of the song, to restore it to its full form. Only then could she hope to use it to communicate with the spirits and unlock the secrets of the veil.

The decision filled her with both excitement and trepidation. The forest was vast, and the task before her was daunting. But Elara was no stranger to challenges, and the call of the song was too strong to ignore. She would embark on this quest, and she would not stop until she had found every missing piece of the song.

Elara spent the rest of the day preparing for her journey. She packed a small satchel with provisions—a loaf of bread, a flask of water, some dried fruits—and the talisman that Lysandra had given her. She also took a small notebook and a piece of charcoal, tools she would use to record the fragments of the song as she found them.

As the sun dipped below the horizon, casting long shadows across the village, Elara slipped away from her home and made her way to the edge of the forest. The night was cool and clear, the full moon hanging low in the sky, its light illuminating the path before her.

The forest greeted her with its familiar embrace, the trees closing in around her, their branches intertwining overhead to form a canopy that blocked out the sky. The air was thick with the scent of earth and moss, and the sounds of the night—the rustle of leaves, the chirping of crickets—filled the air. But beneath it all, Elara could hear the melody, faint and elusive, guiding her deeper into the forest.

Elara moved quickly, her steps light and sure as she followed the song. The path she took was not one she had traveled before, but it felt right, as if the forest itself was leading her to where she needed to go. The further she went, the louder the melody became, each note echoing in her mind like a distant memory.

She walked for what felt like hours, the forest around her growing darker and denser with each passing minute. But Elara was not afraid. The song was a beacon, guiding her through the shadows, urging her onward. And then, finally, she came to a stop.

Before her lay a small glade, bathed in the soft light of the moon. The trees here were ancient, their trunks thick and gnarled, their branches reaching high into the sky. In the center of the glade stood a large stone, its surface smooth and polished, as if it had been shaped by human hands. And etched into the stone were symbols—ancient runes that glowed faintly in the moonlight.

Elara approached the stone, her heart pounding with anticipation. She ran her fingers over the runes, tracing their intricate patterns, feeling a connection to the past as she did so. The song was stronger here, clearer, as if the stone itself was singing to her.

She reached into her satchel and pulled out her notebook and charcoal, quickly sketching the runes and noting down the fragment of the melody that echoed in her mind. The notes came easily, flowing from her hand as if they had always been a part of her.

As she finished, Elara took a step back and looked at what she had written. The fragment of the song was beautiful, haunting in its simplicity, but it was still incomplete. There were more pieces to find, more notes to uncover.

Elara knew that this was only the beginning. The forest held more secrets, more fragments of the song that would lead her to the truth. She could feel it in her bones, a certainty that drove her onward.

She spent the next several nights venturing deeper into the forest, following the melody wherever it led her. Each time she found a new fragment, it felt like a small victory, a step closer to completing the song. The pieces were scattered across the forest, hidden in the most unlikely of places—carved into the bark of ancient trees, etched into the stones of forgotten ruins, whispered in the winds that swept through the valleys.

As Elara gathered the fragments, she began to notice patterns in the melody, themes that repeated and evolved, creating a complex and intricate composition. The song was not just a means of communication; it was a story, a history of the Night Spirits and their connection to the veil.

The more she uncovered, the more Elara began to understand the spirits. They were not the malevolent beings that some of the villagers feared, nor were they simple guardians of the forest. They were ancient and wise, beings of pure energy who had once roamed freely between the realms, bound by a deep sense of duty to protect the balance between worlds.

But there was also a sadness in the song, a lament for a time long past, when the spirits had been free to move between realms, before the veil had been woven to separate them from the mortal world. The song spoke of loss and longing, of a desire to reconnect with the world they had once known.

As Elara pieced together the fragments, she felt a growing empathy for the spirits. They were not so different from her, beings caught between two worlds, yearning for understanding and connection. The prophecy that Lysandra had spoken of began to take on new meaning. Perhaps the breach of the veil was not about destruction, but about healing—about finding a way to bridge the gap between worlds and restore the balance that had been lost.

But even as Elara grew closer to completing the song, she knew that the final piece was still missing. The melody was beautiful, but it lacked an ending, a resolution that would tie everything together. Without it, the song was incomplete, and its true power remained just out of reach.

One night, as Elara stood at the edge of a cliff overlooking a vast expanse of forest, she heard the song more clearly than ever before. The melody echoed in the wind, carried on the breeze like a whisper from the past. But this time, there was something different—a new note, one she had not heard before.

Elara's heart raced as she followed the sound, her steps quick and determined. The song led her to a narrow path that wound down the side of the cliff, treacherous and steep, but Elara did not hesitate. She had come too far to turn back now.

The path led her to a hidden cave, its entrance obscured by a curtain of ivy and moss. The song was louder here, resonating from within the depths of the cave, calling to her with an urgency she could not ignore.

Elara pushed aside the ivy and stepped into the cave, her breath catching in her throat as she took in the sight before her. The walls of the cave were lined with crystals, their surfaces glowing with a soft, ethereal light that illuminated the entire space. And at the far end of the cave, resting on a pedestal of stone, was a small, intricately carved wooden box.

Elara approached the box, her heart pounding in her chest. The song was almost deafening now, each note vibrating through her entire being. She reached out with trembling hands and lifted the lid of the box.

Inside was a single sheet of parchment, yellowed with age but still intact. The parchment was covered in the same ancient runes that Elara had seen on the stone in the glade, and as she looked closer, she saw that they formed the final verses of the song.

Elara carefully lifted the parchment from the box, her hands shaking with excitement. She had found it—the missing piece, the final verses that would complete the song and unlock its full power.

She quickly pulled out her notebook and began to copy the runes, her heart racing as the melody filled her mind. The notes flowed from her hand, each one fitting perfectly into the melody she had already pieced together. As she wrote, the song began to take shape in her mind, complete and whole for the first time.

When she finished, Elara stepped back and looked at what she had written. The song was beautiful, a masterpiece of harmony and emotion that resonated deep within her soul. But more than that, it was powerful. She could feel the energy emanating from the notes, a connection to the spirits that was stronger than anything she had ever felt before.

With the song complete, Elara knew that she was ready to use it. She could now communicate with the Night Spirits, understand their language, and unlock the secrets of the veil. But she also knew that this was only the beginning. The prophecy was still unfulfilled, and the path ahead was uncertain.

As Elara left the cave and made her way back up the cliff, the song played in her mind, each note a reminder of the power she now held. She felt a sense of clarity and purpose, a determination to see this journey through to the end.

When she reached the top of the cliff, Elara paused and looked out over the forest. The moon hung low in the sky, casting its silver light over the treetops, and the wind carried the faint echoes of the song through the air.

Elara took a deep breath and closed her eyes, letting the melody fill her mind. She could feel the presence of the spirits all around her, their energy intertwined with the song, their voices now clear and understandable.

It was time.

Elara opened her eyes and began to sing, her voice carrying the melody through the night. The song flowed from her like a river, each note resonating with the spirits, drawing them closer. As she sang, she felt a connection to the spirits, a bond that transcended the boundaries of the veil.

The forest around her came alive with energy, the trees swaying in time with the melody, the leaves rustling like a chorus of whispers. The spirits emerged from the shadows, their forms shifting and ethereal, their eyes glowing with an otherworldly light.

Elara continued to sing, her voice growing stronger with each verse. The spirits moved closer, drawn to the song, their movements graceful and fluid. They danced around her, their forms weaving in and out of the light, their energy merging with hers.

As the final notes of the song echoed through the forest, the spirits came to a stop, their eyes fixed on Elara. There was a moment of silence, a pause as the energy in the air reached its peak.

And then, the spirits spoke.

Their voices were soft and melodic, their language a blend of tones and harmonies that Elara could now understand. They thanked her for completing the song, for restoring the connection between the realms. They spoke of the prophecy, of the role she was destined to play in restoring the balance between worlds.

But they also spoke of the dangers that lay ahead, of the forces that would seek to disrupt the balance and prevent the prophecy from being fulfilled. They warned Elara that her journey was far from over, that the true test was still to come.

Elara listened, her heart heavy with the weight of their words. She knew that the path ahead would be difficult, but she was ready. She had the song, the key to understanding the spirits and the veil, and she would use it to fulfill her destiny.

As the spirits began to fade back into the shadows, Elara felt a sense of calm settle over her. The song had given her the strength and clarity she needed to face the challenges ahead, and she was determined to see her journey through to the end.

She turned and made her way back to the village, the song still playing in her mind, a reminder of the power she now held. The forest was quiet as she walked, the whispers now a gentle hum that accompanied her every step.

When Elara reached the edge of the forest and looked out over the village, she felt a renewed sense of purpose. The prophecy was no longer just a distant possibility—it was her reality, and she would do whatever it took to fulfill it.

With the song of the spirits now complete, Elara knew that she had the power to bridge the gap between worlds, to restore the balance that had been lost. But she also knew that this power came with great responsibility, and that the choices she made in the days to come would determine the fate of both realms.

As she stepped into the light of the village, Elara felt a sense of peace and clarity that she had not felt in a long time. The path ahead was still uncertain, but she was no longer afraid. She had the song, the spirits, and the strength within her to face whatever challenges lay ahead.

And she would not stop until the prophecy was fulfilled, until the balance between worlds was restored, and the veil was healed.

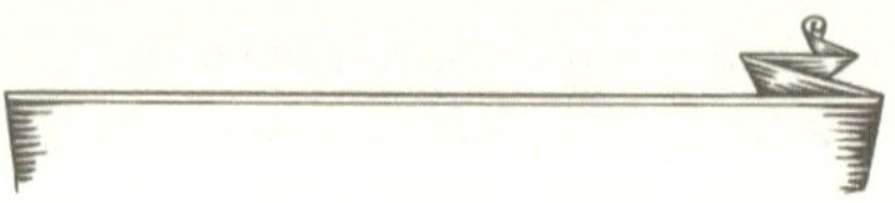

Chapter 8: The Trials of the Moonlit Path

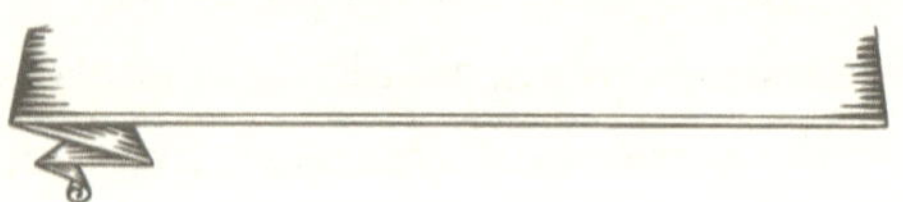

The Moonlit Veil had always been a place of wonder and mystery, but now it was also a place of danger. Elara had spent countless nights navigating the Whispering Forest, uncovering the fragments of the ancient song that allowed her to understand the language of the Night Spirits. The song was her key to bridging the gap between the mortal world and the realm of the spirits, but it was also the key to something much more profound and perilous. The spirits had warned her of the dangers that lay ahead, and now, as she ventured deeper into the forest, she could feel those dangers looming closer.

Elara knew that the path before her would not be easy. The Night Spirits had set trials in her way, tests of her courage, wisdom, and heart. She could sense that each trial was designed to challenge her in ways she could not yet imagine, to push her to her limits and reveal the truth of her character. But she also knew that these trials were necessary. Only by proving her worthiness could she hope to fulfill the prophecy and restore the balance between the realms.

The moon was high in the sky as Elara made her way through the forest, its silver light casting long shadows on the ground. The air was cool and crisp, filled with the scent of pine and earth. The forest was alive with the sounds of the night—crickets chirping, leaves rustling in the breeze, the distant call of an owl—but beneath it all, Elara could hear the whispers of the Night Spirits, guiding her toward her first trial.

The path she followed was unfamiliar, winding through dense thickets and over rocky terrain. The trees seemed to close in around her, their branches reaching out like skeletal hands. But Elara pressed on, her heart steady and her mind focused. She had come too far to turn back now.

After what felt like hours of walking, Elara emerged into a clearing bathed in the soft glow of the moonlight. The clearing was surrounded by tall, ancient trees, their trunks gnarled and twisted with age. In the center of the clearing stood a large stone altar, its surface worn smooth by centuries of wind and rain. The altar was adorned with symbols and runes, the same ancient language that Elara had seen before, etched into the stone with a precision that spoke of both reverence and power.

Elara approached the altar cautiously, her heart pounding in her chest. She could feel the presence of the spirits all around her, their energy humming in the air like a chorus of whispers. The first trial was about to begin.

As Elara stood before the altar, the air around her grew still, the sounds of the night fading into silence. The light of the moon seemed to intensify, casting the clearing in an ethereal glow. And then, from the shadows at the edge of the clearing, a figure emerged.

The figure was tall and cloaked in darkness, their form shifting and insubstantial, as if they were made of shadow and moonlight. Their eyes glowed with a soft, silvery light, and as they moved closer, Elara could see that their features were both familiar and alien—a reflection of the forest itself, ancient and wise.

"Elara," the figure spoke, their voice a melodic whisper that seemed to resonate with the very air around them. "You have come far, but your journey is only beginning. The trials of the Moonlit Path are not for the faint of heart. They will test you in ways you cannot yet imagine, and you must be prepared to face your deepest fears and desires."

Elara swallowed hard, her hands trembling slightly at her sides. "I understand," she said, her voice steady despite the fear gnawing at her insides. "I'm ready."

The figure nodded, their gaze piercing as they regarded her. "Very well. The first trial is one of courage. You must face the darkness within yourself and conquer the fears that have held you back. Only then can you move forward on this path."

As the figure spoke, the clearing around Elara began to change. The trees seemed to grow taller and darker, their branches twisting into grotesque shapes. The ground beneath her feet became uneven and treacherous, and the light of the moon dimmed, casting the world into shadow. The air grew cold, and a sense of foreboding settled over the clearing like a heavy blanket.

Elara took a deep breath, steeling herself for what was to come. She knew that the trial would not be easy, but she also knew that she could not turn back. She had faced darkness before—both in the forest and within herself—and she was determined to overcome whatever challenges the spirits had in store for her.

The figure gestured toward the shadows at the edge of the clearing. "Enter the darkness, Elara. Face your fears, and find the light within."

Elara nodded, her resolve firm. She stepped forward, her feet carrying her toward the shadows. As she crossed the threshold, the world around her shifted, the clearing fading into darkness until she was surrounded by an inky blackness that seemed to swallow all light and sound. She could no longer see the figure or the altar, and the whispers of the spirits had fallen silent.

For a moment, Elara stood frozen, her heart racing in her chest. The darkness was suffocating, pressing in on her from all sides. But she knew that she could not let fear control her. She had to move forward, to find her way through the darkness and complete the trial.

Taking a deep breath, Elara began to walk. The ground beneath her feet was uneven, and she stumbled several times, but she forced herself to keep going. The darkness was disorienting, and it was difficult to tell which direction she was moving in. But Elara knew that she had to trust herself, to rely on her instincts and the strength within her.

As she walked, the darkness seemed to grow thicker, the air around her heavy and oppressive. Elara could feel her fear rising, threatening to overwhelm her. But she pushed it down, focusing on the light she knew was within her, the light that had guided her through so many challenges before.

The trial was not just about facing external dangers; it was about confronting the darkness within herself—the doubts, the fears, the insecurities that had haunted her for so long. Elara had always been brave, but there were times when she had doubted herself, when she had feared that she was not strong enough to fulfill her destiny. Those fears were now manifesting in the darkness around her, threatening to consume her.

But Elara was determined to overcome them. She would not allow fear to dictate her path. She would find the light, no matter how deep the darkness.

As she continued to walk, Elara began to notice small glimmers of light in the distance, faint and flickering like stars in the night sky. The lights were far apart, and it was difficult to tell how close they were, but Elara knew that they were the key to completing the trial. She had to reach them, to gather them and bring them together.

The closer she got to the lights, the more intense the darkness became. It pressed in on her from all sides, cold and unyielding. But Elara did not waver. She focused on the light, using it as a guide, and pushed forward.

The first light was closer than she had expected, a small, glowing orb suspended in the air like a beacon. Elara reached out and touched it, feeling its warmth spread through her fingers. The light pulsed, growing brighter as she held it, and she could feel a sense of calm and strength wash over her.

With the light in hand, the darkness around her seemed to retreat slightly, the shadows growing less oppressive. Elara knew that she had to find the other lights, to gather them and bring them together. Only then would she be able to overcome the darkness and complete the trial.

She continued to move forward, her steps more confident now. The next light was further away, but Elara could see it glowing faintly in the distance. She moved toward it, her determination unwavering, and reached out to grasp it.

As she did, the darkness around her seemed to shift, growing more intense, as if it were trying to prevent her from reaching the light. But Elara was not deterred. She reached out with both hands, grasping the light and pulling it toward her. The darkness pushed back, cold and unyielding, but Elara's strength held firm. The second light pulsed and grew brighter, joining the first in her hands.

With two lights in hand, the darkness around her seemed to retreat even further, the shadows growing less menacing. Elara could see the path ahead more clearly now, illuminated by the combined glow of the lights she held. But she knew that the trial was not yet over. There were still more lights to find, more darkness to overcome.

The final light was the furthest away, its glow faint and flickering like a dying ember. Elara moved toward it, her heart pounding in her chest. The darkness around her grew denser with each step, the cold biting at her skin, but she pressed on.

As she neared the light, the darkness seemed to gather around it, forming a barrier of shadows that blocked her path. Elara could feel her fear rising again, the doubts and insecurities threatening to overwhelm her. But she knew that she could not give in. She had to reach the light, to bring all three together and banish the darkness once and for all.

She took a deep breath, steeling herself, and pushed forward. The darkness pushed back, cold and unyielding, but Elara's determination held firm. She reached out with both hands, grasping the light and pulling it toward her. The shadows clung to her, cold and suffocating, but Elara's strength did not waver.

With a final surge of effort, Elara pulled the third light toward her, joining it with the others. The moment the three lights came together, they pulsed with a brilliant, blinding light, banishing the darkness and illuminating the world around her.

Elara stood in the clearing once more, the darkness gone, the altar and the figure before her bathed in the soft glow of the moonlight. The trial was over.

The figure regarded her with a look of approval. "You have faced the darkness within yourself and conquered your fears. You have proven your courage, Elara, and you are one step closer to fulfilling your destiny."

Elara nodded, feeling a sense of accomplishment and relief wash over her. The first trial had been difficult, but she had overcome it. She had faced her fears and emerged stronger for it.

But as the figure spoke, Elara could feel the energy in the air shift, the whispers of the spirits growing louder. The next trial was about to begin.

"The second trial is one of wisdom," the figure said, their voice steady and measured. "You must navigate the maze of the mind and find the truth within the labyrinth of your thoughts. Only by understanding the true nature of your thoughts and beliefs can you move forward on this path."

As the figure spoke, the world around Elara began to change once more. The clearing faded away, replaced by a vast, intricate maze of twisting corridors and winding paths. The walls of the maze were high and imposing, made of smooth stone that seemed to pulse with a faint, ethereal light. The air was thick with the scent of earth and stone, and the whispers of the spirits echoed through the maze, guiding Elara deeper into its depths.

Elara knew that this trial would be different from the first. It was not about facing external dangers, but about navigating the complexities of her own mind—her thoughts, beliefs, and perceptions. She had to find her way through the maze, to uncover the truth that lay at its center.

Taking a deep breath, Elara stepped forward, her heart steady and her mind focused. The path before her was winding and uncertain, but she knew that she had to trust herself, to rely on her intuition and wisdom to guide her.

As she walked, the whispers of the spirits grew louder, echoing through the maze like a chorus of voices. The whispers were soft and melodic, their language a blend of tones and harmonies that Elara could now understand. They spoke of the nature of thought, of the illusions and deceptions that often cloud the mind, and of the importance of seeing through those illusions to uncover the truth.

The path was not easy. The maze was filled with dead ends and false leads, and more than once, Elara found herself back at the beginning, forced to start over. But she did not give up. Each time she reached a dead end, she paused, reflecting on the thoughts and beliefs that had led her there, and adjusted her course.

As she navigated the maze, Elara began to understand the nature of the trial. The maze was not just a physical structure; it was a reflection of her own mind, a representation of the thoughts and beliefs that guided her actions. The dead ends and false leads were the illusions and deceptions that had clouded her judgment, and the true path was the one that led to clarity and understanding.

The further she went, the more complex the maze became. The walls grew higher, the corridors narrower, and the whispers louder. But Elara remained focused, using her intuition and wisdom to guide her.

Finally, after what felt like hours of walking, Elara reached the center of the maze. There, in the heart of the labyrinth, she found a small, circular chamber bathed in the soft glow of the moonlight. In the center of the chamber stood a pedestal, and on it rested a small, intricately carved wooden box.

Elara approached the box cautiously, her heart pounding in her chest. She could feel the energy in the air, the whispers of the spirits growing louder as she drew closer. The box was the key to the trial, the truth that lay at the heart of the maze.

She reached out and lifted the lid of the box, her hands trembling slightly. Inside was a single sheet of parchment, yellowed with age but still intact. The parchment was covered in the same ancient runes that Elara had seen before, and as she looked closer, she saw that they formed a riddle.

The riddle was simple yet profound, a question that cut to the heart of the trial: *What is the true nature of your thoughts?*

Elara pondered the question, her mind racing with possibilities. The maze had been a reflection of her own mind, a representation of the thoughts and beliefs that guided her actions. The dead ends and false leads had been the illusions and deceptions that had clouded her judgment. But what was the true nature of her thoughts?

As she stood there, reflecting on the question, the answer came to her with a clarity that was almost startling. The true nature of her thoughts was not in the thoughts themselves, but in the awareness that observed them. The thoughts were like clouds passing through the sky, temporary and fleeting, but the awareness that observed them was constant and unchanging.

With that realization, the riddle seemed to dissolve in her mind, and the maze around her began to fade. The walls of the labyrinth melted away, and Elara found herself back in the clearing, standing before the altar and the figure.

The figure regarded her with a look of approval. "You have navigated the maze of your mind and uncovered the truth within. You have proven your wisdom, Elara, and you are one step closer to fulfilling your destiny."

Elara nodded, feeling a sense of accomplishment and clarity wash over her. The second trial had been challenging, but she had emerged stronger for it. She had navigated the complexities of her own mind and uncovered the truth that lay at its center.

But as the figure spoke, Elara could feel the energy in the air shift once more, the whispers of the spirits growing louder. The final trial was about to begin.

"The third and final trial is one of the heart," the figure said, their voice steady and measured. "You must confront the deepest desires and fears of your heart and find the strength to choose the path of compassion and love. Only by opening your heart to the truth can you move forward on this path."

As the figure spoke, the world around Elara began to change once more. The clearing faded away, replaced by a vast, open landscape bathed in the soft glow of the moonlight. The landscape was both familiar and alien, a reflection of the deepest parts of Elara's heart—the places where her desires, fears, and emotions resided.

Elara knew that this trial would be the most challenging of all. It was not about facing external dangers or navigating the complexities of her mind; it was about confronting the deepest parts of herself—the desires and fears that had shaped her actions and guided her path.

Taking a deep breath, Elara stepped forward, her heart steady and her mind focused. The path before her was uncertain, but she knew that she had to trust herself, to rely on the strength of her heart to guide her.

As she walked, the landscape around her shifted and changed, reflecting the emotions and desires that resided within her. There were moments of joy and peace, where the landscape was filled with vibrant colors and blooming flowers, and there were moments of fear and doubt, where the landscape was dark and barren, the ground cracked and dry.

Elara confronted each emotion and desire as it arose, reflecting on its nature and the role it had played in her life. She acknowledged the joy and peace, allowing herself to feel the warmth and love that filled her heart. But she also confronted the fear and doubt, allowing herself to feel the pain and sorrow that had shaped her actions.

The trial was not about denying her emotions or suppressing her desires; it was about embracing them, understanding them, and finding the strength to choose the path of compassion and love.

As Elara continued to walk, she reached a point where the landscape became dark and stormy, the sky filled with swirling clouds and the ground trembling beneath her feet. She could feel the weight of her fears pressing down on her, the doubts and insecurities that had haunted her for so long.

But in the midst of the storm, Elara found the strength within her heart to rise above the fear. She focused on the light that had guided her through the previous trials, the light of compassion and love that resided within her.

With that strength, Elara reached out and touched the storm, allowing the light of her heart to flow through her. The storm began to calm, the clouds parting to reveal a clear, starry sky. The ground beneath her feet steadied, and the landscape began to transform, the darkness giving way to light, the barren ground blooming with flowers once more.

Elara had completed the final trial. She had confronted the deepest parts of herself and found the strength to choose the path of compassion and love.

As the landscape around her faded, Elara found herself back in the clearing, standing before the altar and the figure. The figure regarded her with a look of deep respect and approval.

"You have faced the trials of the Moonlit Path and proven your worthiness," the figure said, their voice filled with reverence. "You have shown courage, wisdom, and heart, and you are now ready to fulfill your destiny."

Elara nodded, feeling a sense of peace and clarity wash over her. The trials had been difficult, but she had emerged stronger for them. She had faced her fears, navigated the complexities of her mind, and opened her heart to the truth.

The path ahead was still uncertain, but Elara knew that she was ready to face whatever challenges lay ahead. She had the strength within her to fulfill the prophecy, to restore the balance between worlds, and to heal the veil.

As the figure began to fade, their form dissolving into the moonlight, Elara felt a sense of gratitude and reverence for the spirits that had guided her on this journey. She had come so far, and there was still so much more to do, but she knew that she was not alone. The spirits were with her, their whispers a constant presence in her mind, guiding her every step of the way.

With a deep breath, Elara turned and made her way back through the forest, the light of the moon illuminating the path before her. The night was quiet and still, the air filled with the scent of pine and earth. The trials had been completed, but the journey was far from over.

As she reached the edge of the forest and stepped into the light of the village, Elara felt a renewed sense of purpose and determination. The veil still called to her, its whispers a reminder of the prophecy she was destined to fulfill. But now, she had the strength and clarity to face whatever challenges lay ahead.

With the trials of the Moonlit Path behind her, Elara was ready to continue her journey, to unlock the secrets of the veil, and to restore the balance between worlds.

And she would not stop until her destiny was fulfilled.

Chapter 9: The Betrayal of the Veil

The Whispering Forest had always been a place of secrets, its ancient trees and winding paths concealing mysteries that spanned centuries. But never had the forest felt so ominous, so fraught with danger, as it did now. The trials of the Moonlit Path had strengthened Elara, revealing the depths of her courage, wisdom, and heart. But as she emerged from those trials, the world she returned to seemed darker, more precarious than before. Something was wrong—terribly wrong.

It began as a subtle shift in the air, a tension that crackled like static electricity. The Night Spirits, usually a calm, guiding presence, had grown restless, their whispers no longer gentle but urgent, tinged with a fear that Elara had never sensed before. The forest, once her sanctuary, now felt like a place on the brink of disaster, its harmony disrupted by a force that Elara could not yet identify.

Returning to the village, Elara tried to shake off the unease that had settled over her, but it clung to her like a shadow. The villagers went about their daily lives as usual, seemingly unaware of the impending danger, but Elara could sense it in the way the animals behaved, in the unnatural silence that fell over the village at dusk, in the way the wind seemed to carry whispers of warning through the trees.

It wasn't long before Elara's worst fears were confirmed.

One evening, as she was preparing to leave her home and return to the forest, Elara overheard a conversation that sent a chill down her spine. She had been gathering supplies when she caught sight of two villagers speaking in hushed tones outside the blacksmith's shop. Something in their demeanor—the furtive glances, the low voices—caught her attention, and she moved closer, hiding in the shadows to listen.

"You're sure about this?" one of the men whispered, his voice filled with uncertainty.

"Positive," the other replied, his tone confident, almost eager. "This is our chance. If we destroy the veil, we'll have control over both realms—the mortal world and the spirit realm. No one will be able to stop us."

Elara's heart skipped a beat. Destroy the veil? The very idea was unthinkable. The veil was the boundary that protected both realms, the barrier that kept the balance between the living and the spirits. Without it, chaos would reign, and the consequences would be catastrophic.

She had to know more.

Elara stayed hidden, her heart pounding in her chest as she listened to the men continue their conversation. She recognized one of them—Garrick, the village blacksmith. He was a gruff man, known for his skill at the forge, but he had always kept to himself, rarely interacting with the other villagers. The other man was unfamiliar, his face obscured by the shadows.

"How do we destroy it?" the first man asked, his voice trembling with fear and excitement.

"There's a way," Garrick replied. "A ritual. It's ancient, passed down through generations, but it's dangerous. We'll need to be careful, but once it's done, we'll have the power we've always wanted."

Elara's mind raced as she processed their words. A ritual to destroy the veil? How could Garrick know about such a thing? And why would he want to unleash such chaos upon the world?

She knew she couldn't stay hidden any longer. She had to stop them before it was too late.

Without thinking, Elara stepped out of the shadows, her voice strong and steady despite the fear gnawing at her insides. "You can't do this."

The two men whirled around, their eyes widening in shock as they saw her standing there. Garrick's expression quickly turned to anger, his hands clenching into fists.

"Elara," he spat, his voice filled with venom. "You should have stayed out of this."

"I can't," Elara replied, her gaze unwavering. "The veil protects us all—both the living and the spirits. If you destroy it, you'll unleash chaos on both realms. You have no idea what you're dealing with."

Garrick sneered, stepping closer to her. "You think you can stop us? You're just a girl with dreams of spirits and old legends. You don't know what it's like to be powerless, to be at the mercy of forces you can't control. This is our chance to take back control, to become something more."

Elara's heart pounded in her chest, but she stood her ground. "You don't understand. The veil isn't just a barrier; it's a living entity. It maintains the balance between our world and the spirit realm. If you destroy it, you'll destroy that balance, and the consequences will be devastating."

Garrick's eyes narrowed, his anger giving way to a cold, calculating expression. "That's a risk I'm willing to take. I've been studying the old texts, the ancient rituals. I know what needs to be done. And once the veil is gone, we'll have power beyond imagination."

Elara's mind raced as she searched for a way to stop Garrick and the other man. She couldn't let them go through with their plan, but she couldn't fight them alone. She needed help—someone who understood the danger as she did.

Before she could speak again, Garrick moved swiftly, his hand closing around her arm with a grip like iron. "You're not going to interfere, Elara. I won't let you ruin this."

Elara struggled against his grip, fear coursing through her veins. She knew she had to act quickly before Garrick could carry out his plan.

"Let me go!" she demanded, trying to pull away from him.

Garrick's grip tightened, and he leaned in close, his voice a low growl. "You're coming with us, Elara. You're going to witness the ritual, and then you'll understand. There's no going back now."

Panic surged through Elara, but she forced herself to remain calm. She needed to think, to find a way to escape and warn the others. But before she could react, the other man stepped forward, pulling out a length of rope and quickly binding her hands.

Elara struggled against the restraints, but the rope was tight, cutting into her skin. Garrick and the other man exchanged a glance, and then, without another word, they dragged her away from the village, deeper into the forest.

The journey was rough and disorienting, the trees blurring together as they moved swiftly through the underbrush. Elara's mind raced with fear and anger. She couldn't believe that someone from her own village—someone she had known her entire life—could betray the veil, the spirits, and everything the village stood for.

As they ventured deeper into the forest, the whispers of the spirits grew louder, their urgency palpable. They knew something was wrong; they sensed the impending danger. Elara could feel their fear, their desperation, but she couldn't reach out to them, not with Garrick and the other man so close.

Finally, after what felt like an eternity, they reached a small clearing deep within the heart of the forest. The moon hung low in the sky, casting an eerie light over the clearing. At the center of the clearing stood an ancient stone altar, similar to the one Elara had seen during her trials, but this one was cracked and worn, its surface covered in moss and lichen.

Garrick shoved Elara forward, forcing her to her knees before the altar. The other man quickly set to work, pulling out a small bundle of herbs and a silver dagger, both of which he placed on the altar with reverence.

Elara's heart pounded in her chest as she watched them prepare for the ritual. She knew she had to stop them, but with her hands bound and her strength fading, she felt powerless.

Garrick turned to her, his eyes cold and unfeeling. "This is the beginning, Elara. The beginning of a new world, one where we're in control. The spirits have had their time, but now it's ours."

"You're making a terrible mistake," Elara said, her voice trembling with fear and anger. "The veil protects us all. If you destroy it, you'll bring nothing but ruin."

Garrick's lips curled into a sneer. "You don't understand, Elara. The veil is a prison. It keeps us bound to this world, while the spirits have free reign over theirs. But once it's gone, we'll be free to do as we please."

Elara shook her head, her mind racing for a way to stop them. "You're wrong. The veil isn't a prison; it's a bridge. It connects our world to theirs, but it also keeps the balance. Without it, both worlds will fall into chaos."

Garrick ignored her, turning back to the altar. He began to chant in a low, guttural voice, the words of the ancient ritual echoing through the clearing. The other man joined in, their voices rising in unison as the air around them grew thick with energy.

Elara felt a wave of panic wash over her as she realized how close they were to completing the ritual. She had to do something—anything—to stop them. But with her hands bound and her strength fading, she felt powerless.

As the chanting grew louder, Elara closed her eyes and focused on the talisman that Lysandra had given her. She could feel its warmth against her chest, its energy pulsing in time with her heartbeat. The spirits were with her, their whispers a constant presence in her mind.

She had to find a way to reach them, to call out to them for help.

Taking a deep breath, Elara focused all her energy on the talisman, willing it to connect her to the spirits. She could feel their fear and desperation, but she also felt their strength—the same strength that had guided her through the trials of the Moonlit Path.

With every ounce of willpower she had, Elara reached out to the spirits, sending them a silent plea for help. She could feel their presence growing stronger, their energy swirling around her like a protective shield.

And then, something miraculous happened.

The ropes binding her hands suddenly loosened, falling away as if they had been cut by an unseen force. Elara opened her eyes, her heart racing with a mixture of fear and hope. The spirits had heard her plea—they were helping her.

Without wasting a moment, Elara sprang to her feet, grabbing the silver dagger from the altar. Garrick and the other man whirled around, their eyes wide with shock as they saw her standing there, the dagger in her hand.

"Stop this," Elara demanded, her voice filled with determination. "You don't know what you're doing."

Garrick's expression twisted with rage, and he lunged at her, his hands reaching for the dagger. But Elara was faster. She sidestepped his attack and raised the dagger, holding it out in front of her.

"You don't understand, Garrick," Elara said, her voice trembling with emotion. "The veil isn't just a barrier—it's alive. It's a part of both worlds, and if you destroy it, you'll destroy everything."

Garrick sneered, his eyes filled with fury. "You think you can stop me? You're just a child, Elara. You don't have the power to stop what's coming."

Elara tightened her grip on the dagger, her heart pounding in her chest. "I may not have the power to stop you, but the spirits do. And they won't let you destroy the veil."

Before Garrick could react, Elara called out to the spirits, her voice rising above the chanting. "Please, help me! Protect the veil!"

The air around them suddenly grew cold, and the whispers of the spirits filled the clearing, their voices a chorus of urgency and power. The ground beneath their feet trembled, and the trees swayed as if in response to the spirits' presence.

Garrick's expression faltered, and for the first time, Elara saw fear in his eyes. He glanced around, his confidence wavering as the energy in the clearing grew more intense.

"You don't know what you're dealing with, Garrick," Elara said, her voice steady despite the fear gnawing at her insides. "The spirits won't let you destroy the veil. They'll protect it at all costs."

Garrick's gaze flickered to the other man, who had stopped chanting and was now watching the scene with a mixture of fear and uncertainty. "Finish the ritual!" Garrick barked, his voice filled with desperation.

But the other man hesitated, his eyes darting between Elara and the trembling ground beneath them. The power of the spirits was undeniable, and he was clearly beginning to doubt the wisdom of their plan.

Taking advantage of the momentary distraction, Elara moved swiftly, raising the dagger and driving it into the ground at the base of the altar. The blade struck the earth with a sharp crack, and the energy in the clearing surged, a powerful wave of force that sent both Garrick and the other man stumbling backward.

The air around them erupted with light, the spirits' presence becoming visible as they surrounded the altar, their forms shifting and ethereal. The ground trembled violently, and the trees bent as if bowing to the spirits' power.

Garrick scrambled to his feet, his face pale with fear. "No! This wasn't supposed to happen!" he shouted, his voice trembling.

Elara stood her ground, the dagger still embedded in the earth, her heart pounding with a mixture of fear and determination. "It's over, Garrick. The spirits won't let you destroy the veil. You need to stop this before it's too late."

But Garrick's desperation had taken hold, and he refused to listen. He lunged at the altar, his hands reaching for the herbs and relics that had been placed there for the ritual. But before he could touch them, the spirits intervened.

A powerful gust of wind swept through the clearing, knocking Garrick off his feet and sending the relics scattering across the ground. The light surrounding the spirits intensified, and their voices rose in a deafening crescendo, their power surging through the clearing like a tidal wave.

Elara watched in awe as the spirits surrounded the altar, their forms coalescing into a barrier of light and energy. The ground beneath the altar began to glow, and a soft, melodic hum filled the air—a sound that Elara recognized as the song of the spirits.

The spirits were repairing the damage that Garrick and the other man had done, restoring the balance and protecting the veil from harm.

Garrick's eyes widened in terror as he realized that his plan had failed. He stumbled to his feet and turned to flee, but the spirits were faster. A tendril of light shot out from the barrier, wrapping around Garrick and lifting him off the ground. He struggled against the force, but it was no use. The spirits held him fast, their energy pulsing with a power that was beyond anything Elara had ever seen.

The other man, seeing what had happened to Garrick, turned and ran, disappearing into the forest without a second glance. Elara didn't try to stop him—her focus was entirely on the spirits and what they were about to do.

Garrick's face twisted with fear as he realized that he was at the mercy of the spirits. "Please," he begged, his voice trembling. "I didn't know—I didn't understand. Please, let me go!"

The spirits' voices softened, the light surrounding them dimming slightly. Elara could sense their sadness, their disappointment. They had no desire to harm Garrick, but they could not allow him to continue his plans to destroy the veil.

The tendril of light holding Garrick gently lowered him to the ground, releasing its grip. Garrick fell to his knees, gasping for breath, his face pale and his body trembling with fear.

The spirits spoke then, their voices a chorus of wisdom and compassion. "Garrick, you have been blinded by your desire for power. The veil is not something to be destroyed—it is a sacred bond between our realms. By seeking to break that bond, you have put both worlds in jeopardy."

Garrick lowered his head, his shoulders shaking with silent sobs. "I didn't know... I didn't understand. I'm sorry."

The spirits' light dimmed further, their forms becoming softer, more ethereal. "We will spare you, Garrick, but you must leave this place and never return. The veil must remain intact, and the balance between our worlds must be preserved."

Garrick nodded, tears streaming down his face. "I understand. I won't come back. I swear it."

The spirits slowly withdrew, their forms fading into the light of the moon. The barrier of energy around the altar dissipated, and the clearing returned to its normal state, the ground still and the trees standing tall.

Elara watched as Garrick stumbled to his feet, his body trembling with exhaustion and fear. He glanced at her, his eyes filled with a mixture of shame and gratitude, before turning and fleeing into the forest.

Elara stood in the clearing, her heart heavy with the weight of what had just happened. The veil had been protected, but the threat was far from over. There were still those who would seek to destroy it, driven by greed and ambition.

But Elara knew that she would not face this challenge alone. The spirits were with her, their presence a constant source of strength and guidance. And she was determined to fulfill the prophecy, to protect the veil and restore the balance between the mortal world and the spirit realm.

As the first light of dawn began to break over the horizon, Elara turned and made her way back to the village, the song of the spirits echoing in her mind. The journey ahead would be long and difficult, but she was ready to face whatever challenges lay ahead.

With the spirits by her side, Elara knew that she could overcome any obstacle, and that she would not stop until the veil was safe and the balance between worlds was restored.

Chapter 10: The Gathering of the Night Spirits

The night of the full moon had always been a time of both reverence and fear in Elmsworth. For generations, the villagers had spoken of the Night Spirits, ethereal beings that emerged from the veil when the moon was at its fullest, their presence both awe-inspiring and terrifying. But on this particular night, as the full moon climbed higher in the sky, casting its silver light over the world, there was a sense of foreboding that hung in the air—a feeling that something was terribly wrong.

Elara stood at the edge of the Whispering Forest, her heart pounding with a mixture of fear and determination. She could feel the energy in the air, a tangible force that crackled with tension. The spirits were gathering, their whispers growing louder, more insistent, as if they were calling out to her. The events of the past few days had shaken her to the core—the betrayal of the veil, the near destruction at the hands of Garrick, and the growing realization that the prophecy was unfolding. Now, as she prepared to face the greatest challenge of her life, Elara knew that there was no turning back.

The forest was eerily quiet as Elara ventured deeper into its shadowy embrace. The trees, which had always seemed to welcome her, now loomed like dark sentinels, their branches reaching out like skeletal hands. The moonlight filtered through the dense canopy, casting long, ghostly shadows on the ground. Every rustle of leaves, every creak of wood, sent a shiver down Elara's spine, but she pressed on, guided by the whispers of the spirits.

She knew where she had to go. The veil—the boundary that separated the mortal world from the realm of the spirits—lay deep within the heart of the forest, hidden from the eyes of the village. It was a place of ancient power, a place where the veil between worlds was thin, where the spirits could cross over when the moon was full. But now, the veil was weakening, its fabric beginning to tear, and the spirits were no longer content to remain in their own realm.

As Elara walked, the air around her grew colder, and the whispers of the spirits grew louder, more frantic. She could feel their presence all around her, an invisible force that pressed against her from all sides. The spirits were restless, their energy wild and chaotic, as if the very fabric of their existence was coming undone. The prophecy had warned of this—the day when the veil would tear, when the spirits would be unleashed upon the mortal world, and the balance between realms would be shattered.

But Elara was not ready to let that happen. She had come too far, learned too much, to let the prophecy unfold unchecked. She had the strength of the trials behind her, the knowledge of the spirits' song, and the talisman that Lysandra had given her. She had faced her darkest fears, navigated the labyrinth of her mind, and opened her heart to the truth. Now, she had to find a way to restore the balance before it was too late.

Finally, after what felt like an eternity, Elara reached the clearing where the veil lay. The sight that greeted her took her breath away.

The veil, once a shimmering, translucent barrier that pulsed with the soft light of the moon, was now fraying at the edges, its surface marred by jagged tears that oozed with a dark, swirling mist. The spirits, once graceful and serene, now swirled around the clearing like a tempest, their forms shifting and flickering in and out of existence. Their whispers had become a cacophony of voices, a symphony of despair and anger that reverberated through the air, sending shivers down Elara's spine.

The clearing itself had been transformed by the spirits' presence. The ground was cracked and barren, the trees twisted and gnarled, their branches reaching out like claws. The air was thick with the scent of earth and decay, and the light of the moon, which should have illuminated the clearing, seemed to be swallowed by the darkness that surrounded the veil.

Elara's heart raced as she took in the scene before her. The veil was tearing, its fabric unraveling with each passing moment, and the spirits were seeping through, their energy growing stronger as they began to cross into the mortal world. She could feel the power of the spirits, a force that was both awe-inspiring and terrifying, and she knew that if the veil was not restored, the consequences would be catastrophic.

But how could she stop it? How could she mend the veil and restore the balance before it was too late?

Elara took a deep breath, steeling herself for what was to come. She had to think, to find a way to reach the spirits, to communicate with them and find a way to restore the veil. She had the song—the ancient melody that allowed her to understand the language of the spirits—but would it be enough?

As Elara stepped into the clearing, the spirits reacted immediately. Their whispers grew louder, more urgent, and the air around her seemed to vibrate with energy. The spirits began to circle her, their forms shifting and flickering, their voices a chaotic blend of anger, fear, and desperation.

"Elara," they whispered, their voices a chorus of echoes that seemed to come from all directions at once. "Elara, you have come."

Elara nodded, her heart pounding in her chest. "I have come to help," she said, her voice steady despite the fear gnawing at her insides. "I want to restore the veil, to protect both our worlds."

The spirits' voices rose in a cacophony of sound, their forms swirling around her like a storm. "The veil is tearing," they whispered. "The balance is broken. We cannot return."

Elara's mind raced as she tried to make sense of their words. The veil was tearing—she could see that for herself—but why couldn't the spirits return? What had caused the balance to break?

"Please," Elara said, her voice filled with urgency. "Tell me what I need to do. How can I mend the veil and restore the balance?"

The spirits hesitated, their forms flickering as if they were struggling to hold themselves together. Their whispers softened, becoming more focused, more coherent. "The veil is alive," they said, their voices a harmony of sadness and longing. "It is part of both worlds, and it is breaking because the bond between them is weakening."

Elara's breath caught in her throat as she realized what they were saying. The veil was not just a barrier—it was a connection, a bridge between the mortal world and the realm of the spirits. And that connection was breaking, tearing at the fabric of both realms.

"But why?" Elara asked, her voice trembling. "Why is the bond weakening?"

The spirits' voices grew softer, almost mournful. "Because the mortal world is forgetting," they whispered. "Forgetting the old ways, forgetting the balance, forgetting us."

Elara's heart ached as she listened to their words. The villagers had indeed begun to drift away from the old ways, relying more on the tangible, the visible, and forgetting the ancient traditions that had once connected them to the spirits. The rituals, the songs, the respect for the veil—all of these had begun to fade into memory, seen as nothing more than superstitions of a bygone era.

And in doing so, the bond between the worlds had weakened, leaving the veil vulnerable.

Elara felt a surge of guilt and sorrow. She had always felt connected to the spirits, always respected the veil, but she had never realized how fragile that connection truly was. And now, because of that neglect, both realms were in danger.

But there was still hope. There had to be a way to restore the bond, to strengthen the veil and bring balance back to the worlds.

Elara closed her eyes, focusing on the talisman that hung around her neck. She could feel its warmth, its energy, and she knew that it held the key to mending the veil. The talisman was a link between her and the spirits, a symbol of the connection that had once existed between the worlds. And with the song she had learned, she could use that connection to heal the veil.

Taking a deep breath, Elara began to sing.

The song of the spirits flowed from her lips, the ancient melody resonating with the energy of the clearing. The spirits paused in their restless movement, their whispers falling silent as they listened to the song. The notes echoed through the air, weaving together the threads of the broken bond, reaching out to the spirits and the veil itself.

As Elara sang, she could feel the power of the talisman growing stronger, its energy merging with the song, amplifying its effect. The veil, once frayed and torn, began to shimmer with a soft, silvery light. The tears in its fabric slowly started to mend, the swirling mist that had seeped through retreating back into the realm of the spirits.

The spirits, too, began to calm, their forms becoming more solid, more defined. Their whispers became a harmonious chorus, joining with Elara's song, their energy merging with hers to strengthen the veil.

But the process was slow, and Elara could feel the strain on her body and spirit. The bond between the worlds had been weakened for so long, and mending it was no easy task. The spirits were still restless, their energy wild and chaotic, and the veil was still fragile, its fabric barely holding together.

Elara knew that she couldn't do this alone. She needed the help of the villagers, of those who still remembered the old ways, those who still believed in the power of the veil and the spirits. The bond between the worlds could not be restored by one person alone—it had

to be a collective effort, a reawakening of the connection that had once existed between the mortal and spirit realms.

But time was running out. The moon was at its peak, its light casting an eerie glow over the clearing, and the spirits were growing more restless by the minute. The veil was mending, but not quickly enough, and if it tore completely, there would be no way to restore the balance.

Elara's heart raced as she realized what she had to do. She had to call upon the villagers, to bring them to the clearing and have them join in the song. Only by combining their energy, their belief, could they hope to restore the veil and save both worlds.

With a final burst of strength, Elara sang out a note that resonated through the clearing, a call to the villagers, a plea for help. The note echoed through the trees, carried by the wind, reaching out to the village that lay beyond the forest.

"Please," she whispered, her voice trembling with emotion. "Come to the clearing. Help me save the veil."

For a moment, there was silence. The spirits hovered around her, their energy swirling in the air, their forms flickering like candle flames in the wind. Elara's heart pounded in her chest, fear gnawing at her insides. What if the villagers didn't hear her? What if they didn't come?

But then, in the distance, she heard it—a faint sound, growing louder with each passing moment. Footsteps, the rustling of leaves, voices calling out in the darkness. The villagers were coming.

Elara's heart swelled with hope as she saw the first of the villagers emerge from the trees, their faces filled with a mixture of fear and determination. They had heard her call, and they had come.

One by one, the villagers entered the clearing, their eyes widening as they took in the sight of the fraying veil, the restless spirits, and Elara standing at the center of it all, the talisman glowing brightly at her chest. They were hesitant at first, unsure of what to do, but as they saw the spirits' presence and heard the song, something ancient and powerful stirred within them.

They remembered the old ways—the rituals, the songs, the respect for the spirits that had been passed down through generations. And they understood what Elara was asking of them.

Without a word, the villagers joined hands, forming a circle around the veil. Elara continued to sing, her voice growing stronger with the support of the villagers, and one by one, they began to join in, their voices rising in harmony with hers. The song, once a solitary melody, became a chorus, a powerful force that resonated through the clearing, reaching out to the spirits and the veil.

As the villagers sang, the energy in the clearing grew more intense, the air vibrating with power. The spirits, once wild and chaotic, began to calm, their forms solidifying as they joined in the song. The veil, which had been frayed and torn, began to mend more rapidly, the tears in its fabric closing, the dark mist retreating back into the spirit realm.

Elara could feel the bond between the worlds growing stronger, the connection that had once been weakened now being restored. The spirits' presence became more stable, their whispers harmonious rather than frantic. The veil shimmered with a bright, silvery light, its surface smooth and intact once more.

But the work was not yet done. The song had to continue, the bond had to be fully restored, and the balance had to be reestablished. Elara could feel the strain on her body and spirit, but she knew that she had to keep going. The villagers, too, were growing tired, their voices trembling with exhaustion, but they did not stop. They knew what was at stake, and they were determined to see it through.

The moon began its descent, its light slowly fading as the night wore on. The clearing, once a place of chaos and fear, was now filled with a sense of peace and unity. The villagers' voices rose in harmony with the spirits, their energy merging to strengthen the veil and restore the balance.

Finally, as the first light of dawn broke over the horizon, the song reached its climax. The veil, now fully mended, shimmered with a bright, silvery light, its surface smooth and intact. The spirits, their energy calm and stable, hovered around the clearing, their forms solid and serene.

Elara's voice faltered as exhaustion finally overcame her, but the villagers continued to sing, their voices strong and unwavering. The bond between the worlds had been restored, the balance reestablished, and the veil was safe once more.

As the last notes of the song echoed through the clearing, a sense of calm settled over the forest. The spirits, their task complete, began to retreat back into their realm, their forms fading into the light of the veil. The villagers, too, began to lower their hands, their voices falling silent as they realized that the crisis had passed.

Elara fell to her knees, her body trembling with exhaustion, but her heart filled with relief and gratitude. They had done it—they had saved the veil, restored the bond between the worlds, and averted the catastrophe that had loomed so close.

The villagers slowly approached Elara, their faces filled with a mixture of awe and respect. They had seen the power of the veil, the spirits, and the song, and they understood now what Elara had been trying to tell them—that the old ways, the rituals, the respect for the spirits, were not just superstitions of the past. They were a vital part of the balance between their world and the realm of the spirits, a balance that had to be maintained.

As the sun rose over the horizon, casting its golden light over the clearing, the villagers helped Elara to her feet, their hands gentle and supportive. She was exhausted, but she felt a deep sense of fulfillment and peace.

The veil was safe, the balance restored, but Elara knew that their work was not yet done. The villagers had to remember the lessons of this night, to keep the connection between the worlds strong, to maintain the rituals and respect for the spirits that had once been a vital part of their lives.

And Elara, as the keeper of the song, the talisman, and the bond between the worlds, would continue to guide them, to protect the veil, and to ensure that the prophecy was fulfilled—not with chaos and destruction, but with unity and harmony.

As the villagers began to make their way back to the village, Elara stood at the edge of the clearing, her eyes on the veil that shimmered in the light of the rising sun. The spirits were gone now, their presence a distant memory, but she could still feel their energy, their gratitude, and their trust.

The prophecy had been averted, the veil restored, but Elara knew that the journey was far from over. There would be more challenges, more trials, but she was ready to face them, with the strength of the spirits, the villagers, and the song behind her.

With a deep breath, Elara turned and began to make her way back to the village, her heart filled with hope and determination. The night had been long and difficult, but the dawn had brought a new beginning—a chance to restore the balance, to protect the veil, and to ensure that the connection between the mortal world and the realm of the spirits would never be broken again.

Chapter 11: The Song of Unity

The dawn after the gathering of the Night Spirits brought a calm to Elmsworth that had not been felt in generations. The veil had been mended, the balance restored, and the spirits had retreated back to their realm, leaving the village in a state of cautious peace. But as the first light of the new day bathed the world in its golden glow, Elara knew that her journey was far from over.

The song of the spirits still echoed in her mind, its ancient melody filled with secrets she had yet to uncover. She had spent the night mending the veil, singing with the villagers to restore the bond between the mortal world and the realm of the spirits, but the song was not yet complete. There was a final verse, a missing piece of the puzzle that Elara had to find if she was to fulfill the prophecy and lift the curse that bound the spirits to the veil.

Elara had always known that the spirits were not malevolent. They were guardians, protectors of the balance between worlds, but they were also trapped, bound by a curse that had been placed upon them long ago. The veil, which was meant to be a bridge between realms, had become a prison, keeping the spirits from crossing over, from finding peace. And now, with the veil mended but still fragile, Elara knew that she had to find a way to free them.

The answer lay in the song—the ancient melody that had been passed down through generations, the key to understanding the language of the spirits. But the song was incomplete, and Elara had to find the missing verse, the final piece that would unlock the secrets of the curse and reveal the path to lifting it.

As the villagers returned to their daily lives, their hearts lighter after the events of the night, Elara set out on her own journey. She knew that the answers she sought would not be found in the village, but in the depths of the

Whispering Forest, where the veil and the spirits still lingered, waiting for the final verse to be sung.

Elara spent the morning gathering supplies, preparing herself for the journey ahead. She packed a small satchel with food and water, the talisman that Lysandra had given her, and the notebook that held the fragments of the song she had already uncovered. The villagers watched her with a mixture of curiosity and concern, but Elara offered them only a reassuring smile. She had to do this alone.

By midday, Elara was ready. She left the village without a word, her heart steady and her mind focused on the task at hand. The Whispering Forest welcomed her with its familiar embrace, the trees parting as if to guide her on her path. The air was cool and crisp, the scent of pine and earth filling her senses, and the whispers of the spirits were soft and melodic, a gentle hum that resonated with the song in her heart.

Elara walked for hours, her steps light and sure as she followed the trail that led deeper into the forest. She knew where she had to go—the heart of the forest, where the veil was strongest, where the spirits gathered when the moon was full. It was there that she would find the final verse, the key to lifting the curse.

As the sun dipped below the horizon, casting long shadows across the forest floor, Elara finally reached her destination. The clearing where the veil lay was bathed in the soft light of the setting sun, the trees surrounding it like ancient sentinels. The veil itself shimmered with a silvery light, its surface smooth and intact, but Elara could feel the tension in the air, the sense of something unfinished, something waiting to be resolved.

The spirits were there, their forms barely visible in the fading light, but Elara could sense their presence, their energy a constant hum that pulsed through the clearing. They were watching her, waiting for her to make the next move, to sing the final verse of the song.

Elara took a deep breath and stepped into the clearing, her heart pounding with a mixture of fear and determination. She could feel the weight of the prophecy on her shoulders, the knowledge that the fate of both worlds rested in her hands. But she was ready. She had come too far, learned too much, to turn back now.

The clearing was silent as Elara approached the veil, the spirits hovering around her like a protective shield. She could feel their energy, their presence, and she knew that they were not her enemies. They were bound by a curse, trapped in a cycle that had lasted for centuries, and they were counting on her to free them.

Elara reached into her satchel and pulled out her notebook, the pages filled with the fragments of the song she had uncovered. She flipped through the pages, her fingers trembling as she searched for the missing verse, the final piece that would complete the melody.

But the verse was not there. The song was still incomplete, the final notes missing, and Elara's heart sank as she realized that she had no idea where to find them.

She closed her eyes, the weight of the task before her pressing down on her like a heavy burden. She had come so far, but now, at the final moment, she felt lost, unsure of what to do next.

But then, in the silence of the clearing, Elara heard it—a soft, melodic whisper that seemed to come from within her own mind. The song, the missing verse, was there, buried deep within her memory, waiting to be uncovered.

Elara took a deep breath, focusing all her energy on the melody that echoed in her mind. The notes were faint at first, but as she listened, they grew stronger, clearer, until the final verse of the song was fully formed in her mind.

She opened her eyes, the clearing bathed in the soft light of the veil, and began to sing.

The song flowed from her lips like a river, the ancient melody resonating with the energy of the clearing. The spirits, once restless and chaotic, grew still, their forms solidifying as they listened to the song. The veil shimmered with a bright, silvery light, its surface rippling as if in response to the melody.

As Elara sang, she could feel the power of the song growing stronger, its energy merging with the spirits and the veil. The final verse, the missing piece of the puzzle, was the key to lifting the curse, to freeing the spirits and restoring the balance between the mortal world and the realm of the spirits.

But as the final notes of the song echoed through the clearing, Elara felt a deep sense of foreboding. The song was complete, the curse ready to be lifted, but there was a cost—a great sacrifice that had to be made.

The spirits, their forms now fully solidified, hovered around Elara, their voices a soft, melodic harmony that resonated with the song. "Elara," they whispered, their voices filled with sadness and longing. "You have completed the song, and the curse can now be lifted. But to do so, a great sacrifice must be made."

Elara's heart skipped a beat as she realized what they were saying. The prophecy had warned of this—a mortal who would break the curse, but only at the cost of something precious, something irreplaceable.

"What sacrifice?" Elara asked, her voice trembling with fear and uncertainty.

The spirits' voices softened, their forms drawing closer to her. "The curse binds us to the veil, but it also binds you, Elara. You are the bridge between our worlds, the connection that has kept the balance. To lift the curse, you must be willing to give up that connection, to let go of the bond that ties you to both realms."

Elara's breath caught in her throat as she realized the full extent of what they were asking. The connection she felt to the spirits, the veil, the song—it was a part of her, a part of her very soul. To let go of that connection, to break the bond, would be to give up a piece of herself, to lose something that had defined her entire life.

But she also knew that without the sacrifice, the curse would remain, the spirits would continue to be trapped, and the balance between the worlds would never be fully restored. The veil, though mended, would remain fragile, always at risk of tearing again.

Elara felt tears welling up in her eyes as she struggled with the decision before her. The weight of the prophecy, the burden of the song, pressed down on her, and she felt torn between her duty to the spirits and her own fear of losing something so deeply a part of her.

The spirits hovered around her, their presence a comforting warmth that wrapped around her like a protective cloak. "We do not ask this of you lightly, Elara," they whispered. "The choice is yours, and yours alone. But know that if you make the sacrifice, you will be remembered, honored by both realms, and the balance will be restored."

Elara's heart ached with the enormity of the decision before her. She had always known that her connection to the spirits was special, that it had set her apart from the other villagers, but she had never imagined that it would come to this—that she would have to choose between that connection and the fate of both worlds.

But deep down, Elara knew what she had to do. She had come too far, learned too much, to turn back now. The spirits had trusted her, guided her, and now they were asking her to make the ultimate sacrifice—a sacrifice that would free them, restore the balance, and ensure the safety of both worlds.

Elara wiped away the tears that had begun to fall and took a deep, steadying breath. She looked up at the spirits, their forms shimmering with a soft, ethereal light, and nodded.

"I'll do it," she said, her voice trembling but resolute. "I'll make the sacrifice. I'll let go of the bond, the connection between our worlds, if it means lifting the curse and restoring the balance."

The spirits' voices rose in a harmonious chorus, their forms glowing with a bright, silvery light that illuminated the entire clearing. "Thank you, Elara," they whispered, their voices filled with gratitude and reverence. "You have shown great courage, wisdom, and heart. Your sacrifice will be honored by both realms, and the curse will be lifted."

Elara closed her eyes, the weight of the decision settling over her like a heavy blanket. She could feel the bond between herself and the spirits, the connection that had always been a part of her, growing fainter, weaker, as the spirits began to draw away.

The song of the spirits, the melody that had guided her through so many challenges, began to fade, its notes growing softer, more distant, until they were nothing more than a faint echo in the back of her mind.

Elara felt a deep sense of loss as the bond between herself and the spirits was severed, the connection that had once been so strong now nothing more than a memory. The talisman that Lysandra had given her, the symbol of that bond, grew cold against her skin, its power fading as the spirits drew away.

But even as the bond was broken, Elara felt a sense of peace settle over her. The curse was lifting, the spirits were being freed, and the balance between the worlds was being restored. She had fulfilled the prophecy, completed the song, and made the sacrifice that would ensure the safety of both realms.

The clearing grew quiet as the spirits began to fade, their forms dissolving into the light of the veil. The whispers, once a constant presence in Elara's mind, fell silent, leaving only the soft rustle of leaves and the distant call of birds to fill the air.

Elara opened her eyes, the clearing bathed in the soft light of the setting sun. The veil shimmered with a bright, silvery glow, its surface smooth and intact, and Elara knew that the bond between the worlds had been restored.

But as she looked around the clearing, she felt a deep sense of emptiness, a void where the connection to the spirits had once been. The song, the whispers, the presence of the spirits—they were gone, and Elara felt their absence keenly.

She had done what needed to be done, made the sacrifice that had been asked of her, but it had come at a cost—a cost that she would carry with her for the rest of her life.

Elara took a deep breath, the weight of the sacrifice heavy on her heart, but she knew that she had made the right choice. The spirits were free, the veil was safe, and the balance between the worlds had been restored.

As the last light of the sun dipped below the horizon, casting the clearing into twilight, Elara turned and began to make her way back to the village. The path before her was uncertain, the future unknown, but she knew that she would face whatever challenges lay ahead with the same courage, wisdom, and heart that had guided her through the trials of the Moonlit Path.

The bond between the worlds had been severed, the connection to the spirits lost, but Elara knew that she would never forget the lessons she had learned, the sacrifices she had made, and the song that had once resonated so deeply in her heart.

As she stepped out of the forest and into the light of the village, Elara felt a sense of peace and fulfillment wash over her. The journey had been long and difficult, but she had done what needed to be done, and she would carry the memory of the spirits, the veil, and the song with her always.

With a deep breath, Elara looked up at the night sky, the stars twinkling above her like a million tiny lights, and smiled. The prophecy had been fulfilled, the curse lifted, and the balance restored.

And though the bond between the worlds was no more, Elara knew that she would always be connected to the spirits, the veil, and the song—in her heart, in her soul, and in the memory of the sacrifice she had made.

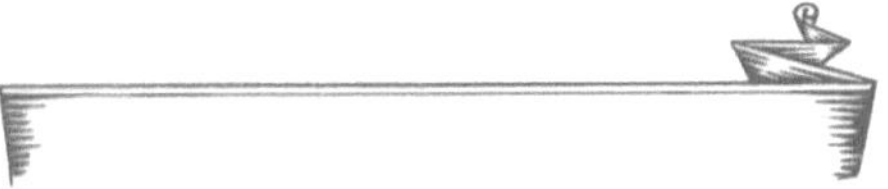

Chapter 12: The Sacrifice of the Veil

The village of Elmsworth had always been a place where stories lived, where legends whispered through the trees and old tales were passed down from generation to generation. But as the full moon rose high in the sky, casting its silver light over the fields and forest, a new story was about to be written—a story of bravery, sacrifice, and the ultimate price of keeping the balance between worlds.

Elara stood at the edge of the Whispering Forest, her heart heavy with the knowledge of what she was about to face. The events of the past days had brought her to this moment, a moment that would determine the fate of the veil, the village, and the realm of the spirits. The final verse of the ancient song had revealed the truth: to lift the curse that bound the spirits and to restore the veil, a great sacrifice was required. And that sacrifice was hers to make.

But there was still one obstacle in her path—the traitor. Garrick, the blacksmith who had once been a trusted member of the village, had betrayed them all. His desire for power had led him down a dark path, one that had nearly destroyed the veil and unleashed chaos on both the mortal world and the realm of the spirits. Even after his initial plan was foiled, Elara knew that Garrick was not finished. He was still out there, somewhere in the forest, waiting for the right moment to strike.

Elara had to stop him. She had to confront Garrick and put an end to his schemes before it was too late. But she also knew that to truly restore the veil and free the spirits, she would have to make the ultimate sacrifice—one that would change her life, and the lives of those she loved, forever.

As Elara stepped into the forest, the whispers of the spirits filled her mind, their voices a chorus of fear and urgency. The veil was weakening again, the bonds that held it together straining under the pressure of the curse. The spirits, once calm and serene, were growing restless, their energy wild and chaotic. Time was running out.

The path through the forest was familiar, but tonight it felt different, more ominous. The trees loomed like dark sentinels, their branches swaying in the wind as if trying to warn her of the dangers ahead. The moonlight filtered through the dense canopy, casting long shadows on the ground that seemed to dance and shift as she walked. Every rustle of leaves, every creak of wood, set her on edge, but she pressed on, guided by the song that still echoed in her heart.

The clearing where the veil lay was silent when Elara arrived. The air was thick with tension, the energy of the spirits palpable. The veil, once a shimmering barrier that pulsed with the light of the moon, was now frayed and torn, its surface marred by dark, swirling mist. The spirits hovered around it, their forms flickering in and out of existence as they struggled to maintain their hold on the mortal world.

But Elara's attention was not on the veil. It was on the figure that stood at the far edge of the clearing, his back turned to her as he stared at the weakened barrier. Garrick.

Elara's heart pounded in her chest as she took a step forward, her voice steady despite the fear gnawing at her insides. "Garrick."

The blacksmith turned slowly, his expression one of cold determination. His eyes, once familiar, now held a hardness that Elara had never seen before. The man who had once been a trusted member of the village was gone, replaced by someone driven by a dark desire for power.

"Elara," Garrick said, his voice low and filled with menace. "I didn't expect you to come alone. But it doesn't matter. This ends tonight."

Elara's grip tightened on the talisman that hung around her neck, its warmth a reminder of the strength she carried within her. "You don't have to do this, Garrick," she said, her voice filled with both pleading and resolve. "The veil is more than just a barrier. It's a bond between our world and the spirits. If you destroy it, you'll unleash chaos on both realms. There's still time to stop this."

Garrick's lips curled into a sneer. "You think I don't know that? The chaos is the point, Elara. With the veil gone, the power of the spirits will be ours to control. The village will bow to us, and the spirits will serve us. We will be gods in our own right."

Elara's heart ached at the madness in Garrick's words. He had been consumed by his desire for power, blinded to the consequences of his actions. But she could still see a flicker of doubt in his eyes, a part of him that remembered the man he once was.

"There's no power in chaos, Garrick," Elara said softly. "Only destruction. The spirits aren't meant to be controlled. They're guardians, protectors of the balance between our world and theirs. If you break that balance, there will be nothing left to rule over."

Garrick's sneer faltered, but only for a moment. His expression hardened, and he took a step toward the veil, his hand reaching for the silver dagger that hung at his side. "I'm done listening to your sermons, Elara. The time for talk is over."

Elara's breath caught in her throat as she realized what he was about to do. The dagger—it was the same one he had used in the failed ritual, the one that had nearly torn the veil apart. If Garrick succeeded in his plan, there would be no coming back. The veil would be destroyed, the spirits unleashed, and the world would be plunged into darkness.

But Elara was not about to let that happen. She had come too far, learned too much, to let everything be undone now. The final verse of the song echoed in her mind, its melody filled with both hope and sorrow. The spirits were counting on her, and she knew what she had to do.

With a deep breath, Elara stepped forward, placing herself between Garrick and the veil. "I won't let you do this, Garrick."

Garrick hesitated, his eyes narrowing as he studied her. "And what are you going to do to stop me, Elara? You're just a girl. You don't have the power to stop what's coming."

Elara met his gaze, her voice steady and resolute. "I may not have the power to stop you, Garrick. But I have the power to save the veil. And I'm willing to do whatever it takes."

Garrick's eyes widened in realization as the meaning of her words sank in. "You can't be serious," he said, his voice trembling with a mixture of fear and disbelief. "You're willing to sacrifice yourself for this?"

Elara's heart ached with the weight of the decision she had made, but she knew it was the only way. "If it means saving the veil, if it means restoring the balance and freeing the spirits, then yes. I'm willing to make that sacrifice."

Garrick's face twisted with anger, his grip tightening on the dagger. "You're a fool, Elara. A naive fool. But if you're so eager to throw your life away, then so be it."

Elara braced herself as Garrick lunged at her, the dagger flashing in the moonlight. But she was ready. With a burst of energy, she raised the talisman to her lips and began to sing.

The song of the spirits flowed from her lips, the ancient melody resonating with the energy of the clearing. The spirits, once restless and chaotic, grew still, their forms solidifying as they listened to the song. The veil, which had been frayed and torn, began to shimmer with a bright, silvery light, its surface rippling as if in response to the melody.

Garrick faltered, the dagger slipping from his grasp as the power of the song washed over him. The force of the spirits' presence, combined with the energy of the song, was too much for him to resist. He stumbled backward, his face pale with fear and confusion.

Elara continued to sing, her voice growing stronger with each note. The final verse of the song, the one that held the key to lifting the curse, filled the clearing with a power that resonated deep within the earth itself. The veil responded, its surface glowing with a radiant light that illuminated the entire forest.

As Elara sang, she could feel the bond between herself and the spirits growing stronger, their energy merging with hers to strengthen the veil. But she also knew that this was the moment of sacrifice—the moment when she would have to let go of the bond, to sever the connection that had been a part of her for so long.

With a final, heart-wrenching note, Elara released the talisman, letting it fall to the ground. The bond between herself and the spirits shattered, the connection that had once been so strong now broken forever. The energy of the song surged through the clearing, and Elara felt a wave of exhaustion wash over her as the sacrifice was made.

The veil, once frayed and torn, was now whole again, its surface smooth and intact. The spirits, their forms solid and serene, hovered around the clearing, their whispers a harmonious chorus of gratitude and peace. The curse that had bound them for so long was lifted, and they were finally free.

But Elara's strength was fading fast. The sacrifice had taken its toll, and she knew that she had given everything she had to save the veil. Her vision blurred as she stumbled forward, her legs trembling with the effort to stay upright.

Garrick, his face filled with a mixture of fear and regret, watched in stunned silence as Elara collapsed to her knees. The power of the song, the spirits, and the veil had been too much for him, and he was left standing there, defeated and broken.

Elara's breath came in ragged gasps as she looked up at the veil, now glowing with a soft, silvery light. The spirits, their energy calm and stable, hovered around her, their forms shimmering in the moonlight. She could feel their gratitude, their relief, and she knew that she had done what needed to be done.

But the cost had been great. The bond between herself and the spirits was gone, the connection that had defined her life now severed. And she was left with nothing but the memory of the song, the sacrifice, and the knowledge that she had saved the village, the spirits, and the balance between worlds.

As the last of her strength faded, Elara closed her eyes, a sense of peace washing over her. The song, the whispers, the presence of the spirits—they were gone, but she knew that she had done what was right. She had fulfilled the prophecy, lifted the curse, and restored the veil.

The villagers would remember her, honor her sacrifice, and the legend of Elara, the girl who saved the veil, would live on in their hearts and minds for generations to come.

With a final, deep breath, Elara let go, her body sinking to the ground as darkness claimed her. The spirits, their forms glowing with a soft, ethereal light, surrounded her, their whispers a gentle lullaby that carried her into the unknown.

And as the moon dipped below the horizon, casting the world into darkness, the clearing grew quiet once more. The veil was mended, the spirits freed, and the balance restored.

But the cost had been great. Elara's bravery, her selflessness, her willingness to sacrifice everything to save the veil, had ensured that the village, the spirits, and the world would be safe. And though she was gone, her memory would live on, immortalized in legend, a shining beacon of hope and courage for all who would come after her.

The sacrifice of the veil was complete, and Elara's story was one that would be told for generations—a story of a girl who, in the face of darkness, chose to be the light.

Chapter 13: The Return of the Guardian

The night had been long, filled with the echoes of ancient songs, the clash of wills, and the ultimate sacrifice that had saved the village of Elmsworth. But as the first light of dawn broke over the horizon, casting a golden glow over the fields and forest, a sense of calm settled over the land. The veil had been mended, the spirits freed from their curse, and the balance between the mortal world and the realm of the spirits restored. The villagers, who had feared for their lives and their future, were now safe once more. But the cost of that safety was still keenly felt in the hearts of those who had witnessed the events of the night.

As the sun rose higher in the sky, the villagers began to emerge from their homes, their faces filled with a mixture of relief and sorrow. The whispers of the night had reached every corner of the village, and by morning, everyone knew of the sacrifice that had been made to save them all. Elara, the young girl who had always felt a connection to the spirits, was gone. Her bravery and selflessness had ensured that the veil was mended, but the loss of her presence was a wound that would take time to heal.

The village square, usually bustling with activity in the early morning, was quiet as the villagers gathered to pay their respects. A somber hush fell over the crowd as they stood together, united in their grief and gratitude. They had all heard the stories of the veil, the spirits, and the prophecy, but none had expected to live through such a legend themselves.

In the midst of their mourning, a figure appeared at the edge of the Whispering Forest, moving with a grace and purpose that immediately drew the attention of the villagers. The figure was tall and cloaked in a deep, midnight blue robe that seemed to shimmer in the morning light. Their face was obscured by the hood of the robe, but as they stepped into the village square, a sense of familiarity washed over the crowd.

The villagers whispered among themselves, some in awe, others in confusion, but all with a deep sense of respect. They knew who this figure was—the guardian of the veil, the ancient protector who had watched over the boundary between worlds for generations. The guardian had been absent during the events of the previous night, but now, with the balance restored, they had returned.

The guardian moved silently through the crowd, their presence commanding without being imposing. The villagers parted to let them pass, their eyes wide with wonder and reverence. The guardian's robe billowed gently in the breeze, the fabric catching the light in a way that made it seem almost otherworldly.

As the guardian reached the center of the village square, they paused, their gaze sweeping over the gathered villagers. Though their face was hidden, there was an unmistakable sense of sadness and understanding in their posture, as if they, too, felt the weight of the sacrifice that had been made.

For a long moment, the guardian stood in silence, the only sound the soft rustling of leaves in the wind. The villagers waited, their breath held in anticipation, knowing that whatever the guardian had to say would be of great importance.

Finally, the guardian spoke, their voice low and melodic, carrying with it the wisdom of countless ages. "People of Elmsworth," the guardian began, their tone filled with both sorrow and reverence, "you have witnessed a great and terrible thing. The veil has been mended, the balance restored, but the price was high. The sacrifice of one who was pure of heart, who understood the true nature of the bond between our worlds."

The villagers bowed their heads, some wiping away tears, others holding their loved ones close. They knew the guardian spoke of Elara, the girl who had given everything to save them.

"The spirits have returned to their realm," the guardian continued, "and the veil is whole once more. But this peace was not easily won. The legend of the Moonlit Veil, the stories of the spirits and the balance, must never be forgotten. For it is in forgetting that we risk losing what has been so dearly regained."

The guardian's words resonated with the villagers, a reminder of the importance of their heritage, of the ancient traditions that had kept the balance for generations. They had become complacent, allowing the old ways to fade into memory, and in doing so, they had nearly lost everything. But now, with the return of the guardian, they were given a chance to right those wrongs, to honor the sacrifices that had been made and ensure that the legend of the Moonlit Veil would endure.

The guardian raised their hands, and a soft light began to emanate from within their robe, casting a gentle glow over the village square. The light was warm and comforting, a balm to the hearts of those who had gathered.

"Elara's sacrifice will not be in vain," the guardian said, their voice carrying a promise of hope and renewal. "She will be remembered, not just as the girl who saved the veil, but as a beacon of courage, wisdom, and love. Her spirit will live on in the stories you tell, in the songs you sing, and in the traditions you uphold."

The villagers nodded, their resolve strengthening in the face of the guardian's words. They would not let Elara's memory fade. They would keep her story alive, passing it down to their children and their children's children, ensuring that the legend of the Moonlit Veil would never be forgotten.

The guardian lowered their hands, the light slowly fading until it was just a soft glow that illuminated the space around them. "The veil is a living thing," the guardian continued, their voice taking on a more instructive tone. "It is not just a barrier, but a bond, a connection between our world and the realm of the spirits. It must be respected, honored, and protected, for without it, both worlds would fall into chaos."

The guardian's gaze swept over the crowd once more, their presence a calming influence on the villagers. "You have a responsibility," they said, their tone firm but kind. "A responsibility to maintain the balance, to keep the old ways alive, and to ensure that the bond between our worlds remains strong. The spirits are not your enemies; they are your allies, your protectors. But they, too, need your respect and your care."

The villagers listened intently, their minds absorbing the wisdom the guardian imparted. They had seen the consequences of neglecting the old ways, of allowing the bond between worlds to weaken. But now, with the guidance of the guardian, they had the chance to make amends, to rebuild that bond and ensure that the veil would remain strong.

The guardian's voice softened, their tone filled with compassion. "I know that you mourn the loss of Elara, and rightly so. But take comfort in the knowledge that her sacrifice was not in vain. She has ensured the safety of your village, of the veil, and of the spirits. Her bravery and selflessness have restored the balance, and for that, she will be honored for all time."

The villagers nodded, their grief tempered by the knowledge that Elara's sacrifice had saved them all. They would carry her memory with them, not just in their hearts, but in the very fabric of their lives.

The guardian stepped forward, moving to the center of the village square where a small stone monument stood. The monument had been placed there many years ago, a simple marker to honor those who had once protected the village from harm. Now, it would serve a new purpose.

With a graceful motion, the guardian raised their hand, and the monument began to glow with the same soft light that emanated from within the guardian's robe. The stone surface shimmered, and slowly, an image began to take shape—a carving of Elara, standing tall and proud, her face filled with determination and strength.

The villagers gasped in awe as the image became clearer, the carving capturing not just Elara's likeness, but her spirit as well. The guardian's light illuminated the carving, making it seem almost alive, a lasting tribute to the girl who had saved them all.

"This monument will stand as a reminder," the guardian said, their voice filled with reverence. "A reminder of the sacrifice that was made, of the bravery and selflessness that saved the veil, and of the importance of maintaining the balance between our world and the realm of the spirits."

The villagers gathered around the monument, their eyes filled with tears of both sorrow and pride. They reached out to touch the stone, their fingers tracing the lines of the carving, feeling the warmth of the guardian's light.

Elara's parents, who had been standing quietly at the edge of the crowd, stepped forward, their faces pale with grief but their hearts filled with pride. They had lost their daughter, but they knew that her sacrifice had been for the greater good. She had become something more than just a girl from the village; she had become a legend.

The guardian turned to face them, their expression hidden but their posture filled with respect. "Your daughter was a beacon of light in a time of darkness," the guardian said, their voice filled with compassion. "Her spirit will live on, not just in this monument, but in the hearts and minds of all who hear her story. She will be remembered for all time as the girl who saved the veil."

Elara's parents nodded, their grief softened by the knowledge that their daughter's sacrifice had made such a profound difference. They stepped forward and placed their hands on the monument, feeling the warmth of the guardian's light and the presence of their daughter's spirit.

The guardian took a step back, their gaze sweeping over the gathered villagers. "The legend of the Moonlit Veil is not just a story," they said, their voice filled with both warning and promise. "It is a reminder of the delicate balance that exists between our world and the realm of the spirits. It is a reminder that we are all connected, and that we must work together to maintain that connection."

The villagers nodded, their resolve strengthened by the guardian's words. They would honor the legend, keep the old ways alive, and ensure that the veil remained strong. They would teach their children the importance of respecting the spirits, of maintaining the balance, and of remembering the sacrifice that had saved them all.

The guardian's presence seemed to grow fainter, the light that surrounded them dimming slightly. "I must return to my duties," the guardian said, their voice soft but firm. "But know that I will always be watching, always protecting the veil and the balance. You are not alone, and as long as you honor the bond between our worlds, the spirits will be your allies, your protectors."

The villagers bowed their heads in respect, their hearts filled with both gratitude and determination. They had been given a second chance, a chance to make things right, and they would not squander it.

The guardian turned and began to walk back toward the Whispering Forest, their robe billowing gently in the breeze. As they reached the edge of the forest, they paused, their gaze lingering on the village, on the monument that now stood as a testament to Elara's bravery and sacrifice.

With a final, graceful motion, the guardian raised their hand, and the light that surrounded them flared brightly for a moment, casting a soft glow over the entire village. The villagers felt a warmth in their hearts, a sense of peace and reassurance, knowing that the guardian would always be watching over them.

And then, with a final whisper of the wind, the guardian disappeared into the forest, their presence fading like a dream at dawn.

The villagers stood in silence for a long moment, their hearts filled with a mixture of emotions. The events of the night had changed them all, had reminded them of the importance of the old ways, of the bond between their world and the realm of the spirits. But they had also been given a gift—the knowledge that they could make a difference, that they could protect the veil and ensure that the balance remained strong.

Elara's sacrifice had been great, but it had not been in vain. Her story would live on, not just in the monument that now stood in the village square, but in the hearts and minds of all who heard it. She had become a legend, a beacon of hope and courage, and her memory would be honored for generations to come.

As the sun rose higher in the sky, casting its warm light over the village, the villagers began to disperse, returning to their homes and their daily lives. But there was a new sense of purpose in their hearts, a determination to honor the guardian's words, to keep the old ways alive, and to ensure that the veil remained strong.

The village of Elmsworth was at peace once more, but it was a peace that had been hard-won, a peace that would be guarded and cherished. The spirits had retreated to their realm, the veil was mended, and the balance was restored. But the memory of the night's events would linger, a reminder of the power of sacrifice, the importance of unity, and the enduring strength of the bond between worlds.

And as the villagers went about their day, they knew that they were not alone. The guardian was watching, protecting the veil, ensuring that the balance remained. And in their hearts, they carried the memory of Elara, the girl who had given everything to save them all.

The legend of the Moonlit Veil would live on, a story of courage, sacrifice, and the power of unity. And as long as that legend was remembered, the village of Elmsworth would remain safe, the veil would remain strong, and the spirits would continue to protect them, just as they had always done.

Chapter 14: The Legacy of the Moonlit Veil

Years had passed since that fateful night when Elara sacrificed herself to mend the Moonlit Veil and restore balance between the mortal world and the realm of spirits. The village of Elmsworth had changed in many ways, but the memory of Elara's bravery and the lessons learned from the events that unfolded remained etched in the hearts of its people. The story of the Moonlit Veil, once whispered as a legend, had become a foundational piece of the village's identity, shaping the way the villagers lived and interacted with the world around them.

The village had grown over the years. New homes were built, families expanded, and children who had only heard the story of Elara in bedtime tales now walked the same paths that she had once tread. But despite the passage of time, the villagers had not forgotten the lessons learned from the Moonlit Veil. They lived in harmony with the Whispering Forest, treating it with the reverence it deserved, aware that the spirits of the forest were their guardians and allies, not to be feared but to be respected.

The forest, once a place of mystery and occasional fear, had become a sanctuary for the villagers. They now understood that the forest was not just a collection of trees and animals, but a living, breathing entity that housed the spirits who had watched over them for centuries. The villagers knew that the veil was a delicate boundary, a sacred site that connected their world to the realm of the spirits, and they honored it with ceremonies, offerings, and visits that kept the bond between the two worlds strong.

The story of Elara had been passed down through generations, told and retold by elders who had been there to witness the events, and by those who had only heard it from their own parents and grandparents. But in each telling, the story remained true to its essence: a tale of courage, sacrifice, and the importance of maintaining the balance between worlds.

Every year, on the night of the full moon closest to the anniversary of Elara's sacrifice, the villagers gathered in the village square to remember her. The ceremony was a solemn yet hopeful occasion, filled with songs, prayers, and stories that celebrated Elara's life and the legacy she had left behind. The villagers would light candles in her honor, placing them at the base of the monument that bore her likeness, a monument that had become a symbol of hope and strength for the entire village.

On the night of the ceremony, the village would be bathed in the soft glow of candlelight, the flames flickering like stars in the darkness. The air would be filled with the scent of incense and fresh flowers, offerings made to the spirits in gratitude for their continued protection. The villagers, young and old, would gather in the square, their voices raised in song as they celebrated the memory of Elara and the bond that had been forged between their world and the realm of the spirits.

The elders of the village, those who had lived through the events of the Moonlit Veil, would take turns telling the story to the younger generations. Their voices, rich with emotion and wisdom, would carry through the night as they recounted the bravery of Elara, the betrayal of Garrick, and the ultimate sacrifice that had saved them all. The children, wide-eyed and filled with awe, would listen intently, their imaginations capturing the magic and mystery of the story.

As the years went by, the story of Elara became more than just a tale of bravery—it became a guide for how the villagers lived their lives. The lessons learned from the Moonlit Veil influenced the way they treated each other, the way they cared for the land, and the way they respected the spirits who watched over them. The villagers understood that the balance between their world and the realm of the spirits was fragile, and that it was their responsibility to maintain that balance, just as Elara had done.

The Whispering Forest, once a place of fear and superstition, had become a sanctuary for those who sought peace, wisdom, and a deeper understanding of the mysteries of the night. The forest was still home to the spirits, and while they remained unseen by most, their presence was felt in every rustle of leaves, every whisper of the wind, and every flicker of moonlight that danced through the trees.

The Moonlit Veil itself had become a sacred site, visited by those who sought to understand the connection between the mortal world and the realm of the spirits. Pilgrims from other villages, drawn by the stories of Elara and the legend of the veil, would make their way to Elmsworth, hoping to catch a glimpse of the veil and to feel the presence of the spirits who guarded it. The villagers welcomed these visitors with open arms, sharing the story of Elara and the lessons they had learned, ensuring that the legacy of the Moonlit Veil would continue to spread far and wide.

The veil, once fragile and torn, was now strong and vibrant, its surface shimmering with a silvery light that pulsed in time with the energy of the forest. The spirits, freed from the curse that had bound them, remained guardians of the veil, their presence a constant reminder of the bond that had been forged between worlds. The villagers knew that as long as they honored the veil, respected the spirits, and lived in harmony with the forest, the balance would remain intact.

But the legacy of the Moonlit Veil was not just about maintaining the balance between worlds—it was also about the importance of courage, sacrifice, and the power of love. Elara's story had become a beacon of hope for those who faced their own challenges, a reminder that even in the darkest of times, one person could make a difference. The villagers carried this lesson with them in their daily lives, drawing strength from the memory of Elara's sacrifice and the knowledge that they, too, could be a force for good in the world.

As the years turned into decades, and the decades into centuries, the village of Elmsworth continued to thrive. New generations were born, grew up, and grew old, but the story of Elara and the Moonlit Veil remained a constant, a thread that wove through the fabric of the village's history. The monument in the village square, once a simple stone carving, had become a place of pilgrimage, a symbol of the enduring legacy of the girl who had saved them all.

The Whispering Forest, though still mysterious, had become a place of refuge for those seeking solace and understanding. The villagers would often walk through its paths, leaving offerings for the spirits and taking a moment to reflect on the lessons of the past. The forest, once seen as a place of danger, was now viewed as a source of wisdom and guidance, a reminder of the connection between all living things.

The full moon, which had once brought fear and uncertainty, was now a time of celebration and remembrance. The villagers would gather to honor Elara and the spirits, lighting candles and singing songs that told the story of the Moonlit Veil. The night was filled with a sense of peace and unity, a reminder that the bond between worlds was strong, and that as long as they continued to honor that bond, the village would remain safe.

But the legacy of the Moonlit Veil was not confined to the village of Elmsworth alone. The story of Elara had spread to neighboring villages, carried by travelers and pilgrims who had heard the tale and been moved by its message. The legend had taken on a life of its own, inspiring others to live with courage, to protect the balance between worlds, and to honor the connection between the mortal world and the realm of the spirits.

In time, the story of Elara and the Moonlit Veil became a part of the broader folklore of the region, a tale told around campfires, in village squares, and in the quiet moments of reflection that followed a long day's work. The story was passed down from generation to generation, its message of hope, sacrifice, and the importance of maintaining balance resonating with all who heard it.

But for the villagers of Elmsworth, the legacy of the Moonlit Veil was more than just a story—it was a way of life. They continued to live in harmony with the forest, mindful of the lessons learned from the legend. The village remained a place of peace and unity, its people committed to honoring the bond between their world and the realm of the spirits.

The veil, now a sacred site, was visited regularly by those who sought to understand the mysteries of the night. Pilgrims from distant lands would come to Elmsworth, drawn by the stories of the Moonlit Veil, hoping to feel the presence of the spirits and to experience the peace that the forest offered. The villagers welcomed these visitors, sharing the story of Elara and the lessons they had learned, ensuring that the legacy of the Moonlit Veil would continue to spread far and wide.

The village square, where the monument to Elara stood, became a place of gathering and reflection. The villagers would often visit the monument, placing flowers and candles at its base, taking a moment to remember the girl who had given everything to save them all. The monument, once a simple stone carving, had become a symbol of hope and strength, a reminder of the power of courage, sacrifice, and love.

As the seasons changed and the years went by, the village of Elmsworth remained a place of harmony and peace. The villagers continued to honor the spirits, to protect the veil, and to live in accordance with the lessons learned from the legend of the Moonlit Veil. The story of Elara, once a tale of mystery and wonder, had become a guiding light for the village, a reminder that even in the darkest of times, there was always hope.

The legacy of the Moonlit Veil had endured, passed down through generations, inspiring all who heard it to live with courage, to protect the balance between worlds, and to honor the connection between the mortal world and the realm of the spirits. The villagers of Elmsworth knew that as long as they continued to live in harmony with the forest, to honor the spirits, and to remember the lessons of the past, the village would remain safe, and the bond between worlds would remain strong.

And so, as the full moon rose high in the sky, casting its silver light over the village and the forest beyond, the villagers of Elmsworth gathered once more to honor the legacy of the Moonlit Veil. They lit their candles, sang their songs, and told the story of Elara, the girl who had saved them all. The night was filled with a sense of peace and unity, a reminder that the bond between worlds was strong, and that as long as they continued to honor that bond, the village of Elmsworth would remain a place of hope, courage, and love.

The legacy of the Moonlit Veil lived on, a beacon of light in the darkness, guiding the villagers of Elmsworth and all who heard its story to live with courage, to protect the balance between worlds, and to honor the connection between the mortal world and the realm of the spirits.

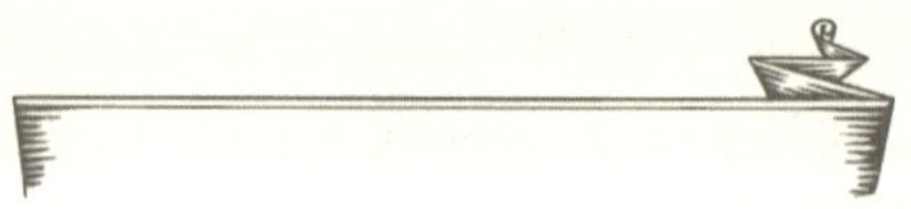

Chapter 15: The New Dawn

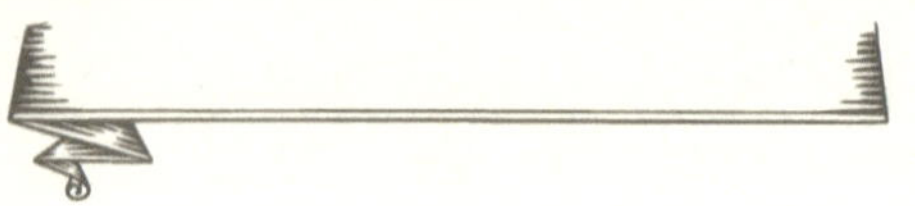

The village of Elmsworth had always been a place where the past and present coexisted in harmony, where the wisdom of ancient stories guided the hands and hearts of its people. As the years passed, the memory of Elara and her sacrifice became more than just a tale told by the elders—it became a living part of the village's soul, woven into the fabric of everyday life. Now, a new generation had come of age, and among them were the descendants of Elara, who bore the weight of her legacy with both pride and humility.

The years had been kind to Elmsworth. The village had grown, its boundaries expanding as more families made their homes there, drawn by the peace and prosperity that seemed to flow from the Whispering Forest. The villagers, guided by the lessons of the past, lived in harmony with the land, nurturing the soil that fed them, respecting the spirits that protected them, and passing down the stories that had shaped their world.

Elara's descendants, now a prominent family in the village, were well aware of the legacy they carried. They knew the story of the Moonlit Veil better than anyone, for it was not just a piece of history—it was their history, a part of their very being. They had inherited not just the blood of the girl who had saved the village, but also her courage, her wisdom, and her deep connection to the spirit realm.

Among Elara's descendants was a young woman named Liora, who bore a striking resemblance to her ancestor. With the same bright eyes and determined spirit, Liora had grown up hearing the stories of her great-great-grandmother, learning from a young age the importance of the bond between the mortal world and the realm of the spirits. She had always felt a deep connection to the Whispering Forest, just as Elara had, and often found herself drawn to the sacred clearing where the veil shimmered in the moonlight.

Liora's parents had raised her with a deep respect for the traditions of the village, teaching her the songs, rituals, and stories that had been passed down through the generations. But more than that, they had instilled in her a sense of duty—a duty to protect the balance that Elara had fought so hard to restore, and to ensure that the legacy of the Moonlit Veil would continue to be honored.

As Liora stood at the edge of the forest, watching the sun dip below the horizon, she felt a familiar sense of peace settle over her. The forest was quiet, the trees standing tall and still, their branches swaying gently in the evening breeze. The air was filled with the scent of pine and earth, a reminder of the life that pulsed through the forest and the spirits that dwelled within it.

Tonight was a special night—the anniversary of Elara's sacrifice, a night when the village would gather to honor her memory and celebrate the bond between worlds. Liora had always looked forward to this night, but this year felt different. There was a sense of anticipation in the air, as if the forest itself was waiting for something to happen.

Liora knew that she had a role to play in the night's events, just as her ancestors had before her. She was the keeper of the stories, the guardian of the songs, and it was her duty to lead the village in their ceremonies, to ensure that the legacy of the Moonlit Veil was honored and that the bond between worlds remained strong.

As the last rays of sunlight faded from the sky, Liora took a deep breath and stepped into the forest, her heart steady and her mind focused. The path to the sacred clearing was one she knew well, but tonight it felt different, more alive. The trees seemed to whisper as she passed, their leaves rustling in a way that was almost musical. The forest, it seemed, was speaking to her, guiding her toward the veil.

When Liora reached the clearing, she paused at the edge, taking in the sight before her. The Moonlit Veil shimmered in the gathering darkness, its surface glowing with a soft, silvery light that pulsed in time with the energy of the forest. The spirits were there too, their forms barely visible, like faint shadows dancing at the edges of her vision. She could feel their presence, a comforting warmth that wrapped around her like a protective cloak.

Liora stepped into the clearing, her movements slow and deliberate, her mind focused on the task ahead. She knew that the villagers would be arriving soon, that they would be looking to her to lead them in the night's ceremonies. But for now, she was alone with the spirits, the veil, and the legacy that had been passed down to her.

As she approached the veil, Liora reached into the pocket of her cloak and pulled out a small, intricately carved wooden box. The box had been passed down through her family for generations, a keepsake that had once belonged to Elara herself. Inside the box was a piece of parchment, yellowed with age but still intact, on which the final verse of the ancient song was written.

Liora had memorized the song long ago, had sung it countless times during the village's ceremonies, but tonight she felt the weight of the words more deeply than ever before. This was not just a song—it was a connection to the past, to the spirits, and to the bond that had been forged between worlds. It was a reminder of the sacrifice that had been made and the responsibility that had been passed down to her.

As the moon began to rise, casting its silver light over the clearing, Liora took a deep breath and began to sing.

The song flowed from her lips like a river, the ancient melody resonating with the energy of the clearing. The spirits, once faint and distant, began to solidify, their forms glowing with a soft, ethereal light that illuminated the entire clearing. The veil, which had been shimmering in the moonlight, seemed to pulse with energy, its surface rippling in response to the melody.

Liora's voice was strong and clear, carrying the weight of the generations that had come before her. The words of the song were familiar, but tonight they felt new, filled with a sense of purpose and power that she had never experienced before. She could feel the connection between herself and the spirits growing stronger, the bond between worlds pulsing with life.

As Liora sang, the villagers began to arrive, their faces illuminated by the light of the candles they carried. They moved silently, gathering around the edge of the clearing, their eyes wide with wonder as they took in the sight of the veil, the spirits, and Liora standing at the center of it all.

The villagers had come to honor Elara, to remember the sacrifice she had made, and to celebrate the bond between their world and the realm of the spirits. But as they listened to Liora's song, they felt something more—an understanding of the legacy they were all a part of, a legacy that had been passed down through generations and would continue to guide them for generations to come.

As the final notes of the song echoed through the clearing, the spirits began to retreat, their forms growing fainter until they were nothing more than shadows at the edge of the veil. The veil itself pulsed with a bright, silvery light, its surface smooth and intact, a symbol of the enduring bond between worlds.

Liora lowered her hands, her voice falling silent as she gazed at the veil, her heart filled with a sense of peace and fulfillment. The song was complete, the connection between worlds restored, and the legacy of the Moonlit Veil honored once more.

The villagers stood in silence for a long moment, their hearts filled with both reverence and gratitude. They had come to honor Elara, but they had also come to reaffirm their commitment to the balance between worlds, to the bond that had been forged so long ago and that continued to guide their lives.

Liora turned to face the villagers, her eyes bright with emotion. "Tonight, we remember Elara," she said, her voice steady and filled with conviction. "We remember her courage, her sacrifice, and the legacy she left behind. But we also honor the bond between our world and the realm of the spirits, a bond that we must continue to protect and respect."

The villagers nodded in agreement, their faces filled with determination. They knew that the legacy of the Moonlit Veil was not just a story—it was a way of life, a guide for how they lived, how they treated each other, and how they interacted with the world around them.

Liora smiled, a sense of pride swelling in her chest as she looked out at the villagers, at the faces of those who had come to honor the legacy she was now a part of. "We are all connected," she continued, her voice filled with warmth and wisdom. "The spirits, the forest, the veil—they are all a part of us, just as we are a part of them. As long as we remember that, as long as we live in harmony with the world around us, the balance will remain, and the bond between worlds will endure."

The villagers began to light their candles, passing the flame from one to another until the entire clearing was bathed in a warm, golden light. The candles, a symbol of the light that Elara had brought into their lives, flickered gently in the night, their flames a reminder of the hope, courage, and love that had saved them all.

As the moon rose higher in the sky, casting its silver light over the village and the forest beyond, Liora led the villagers in a procession back to the village square. The night was filled with the sound of their footsteps, the soft rustle of leaves in the wind, and the distant call of an owl as it flew through the trees.

When they reached the village square, the villagers gathered around the monument that bore Elara's likeness, placing their candles at its base and offering prayers of thanks and remembrance. The monument, now weathered by time but still standing strong, was a testament to the enduring legacy of the girl who had saved them all.

Liora stepped forward, her heart filled with a sense of responsibility and pride as she looked up at the monument. She knew that she was not just honoring the memory of her ancestor—she was continuing the work that Elara had begun, ensuring that the legacy of the Moonlit Veil would live on for generations to come.

As she placed her candle at the base of the monument, Liora felt a sense of peace settle over her. She knew that the path ahead would not always be easy, that there would be challenges and trials just as there had been in the past. But she also knew that she was not alone—that she was surrounded by people who understood the importance of the bond between worlds, who were committed to protecting the balance that had been so carefully restored.

The villagers began to sing, their voices rising in harmony as they celebrated the legacy of the Moonlit Veil. The song, once sung by Elara to mend the veil, had become a symbol of hope, unity, and the enduring connection between their world and the realm of the spirits.

As the song filled the night air, Liora felt a sense of pride and fulfillment wash over her. She had honored the legacy of her ancestor, had fulfilled her duty as the keeper of the stories, and had ensured that the bond between worlds would remain strong.

The night wore on, the villagers continuing to sing, to pray, and to remember the lessons of the past. The candles flickered in the darkness, their flames a reminder of the light that had been brought into their lives by the courage and sacrifice of one girl.

As the first light of dawn began to break over the horizon, the villagers slowly began to disperse, their hearts filled with a sense of peace and renewal.

They knew that the legacy of the Moonlit Veil would continue to guide them, to shape their lives and the lives of their children for generations to come.

Liora remained in the village square, her eyes on the monument as the sun began to rise, casting a warm, golden light over the village. She knew that her work was not done, that there would always be more to learn, more to teach, and more to protect. But she also knew that she was ready for whatever challenges lay ahead.

As the sun climbed higher in the sky, Liora turned and made her way back to the Whispering Forest, her heart filled with a sense of purpose and determination. The forest, now bathed in the soft light of morning, welcomed her with open arms, its trees whispering their secrets as she walked.

When she reached the sacred clearing, Liora paused, her eyes on the veil that shimmered in the morning light. The veil, a symbol of the bond between worlds, stood as a reminder of the legacy she was now a part of, a legacy that would continue to guide her and the villagers for generations to come.

Liora took a deep breath, her heart filled with gratitude and hope as she looked out at the forest, at the trees that had witnessed so much and would continue to stand for generations to come. She knew that she was not alone—that the spirits, the forest, and the legacy of the Moonlit Veil would always be with her, guiding her every step of the way.

As the sun rose higher in the sky, casting its golden light over the village and the forest beyond, Liora smiled, her heart filled with a sense of peace and fulfillment. The new dawn had arrived, and with it came the promise of a future filled with hope, courage, and love.

The legacy of the Moonlit Veil lived on, a beacon of light in the darkness, guiding the villagers of Elmsworth and all who heard its story to live with courage, to protect the balance between worlds, and to honor the connection between the mortal world and the realm of the spirits.

And as the full moon rose once more, casting its silver light over the village and the forest beyond, the Moonlit Veil shimmered in the night, a symbol of the eternal bond between the two worlds.

Don't miss out!

Visit the website below and you can sign up to receive emails whenever Patrick William Lee publishes a new book. There's no charge and no obligation.

https://books2read.com/r/B-A-FLRYB-PJHYE

BOOKS 2 READ

Connecting independent readers to independent writers.

Did you love *The Moonlit Veil*? Then you should read *Tales of the Whispering Forest*[1] by Patrick William Lee!

In "Tales of the Whispering Forest," join Elara and Finn on an epic adventure through a mystical forest filled with ancient secrets and magical beings. From discovering the enchanted grove to uncovering the legend of the Whispering Trees, they face cunning tricksters, powerful witches, and dark forces. Guided by a prophecy, they embark on a quest for the legendary Silver Leaf, unlocking the ability to communicate with the forest and confronting ultimate challenges that test their bravery, wisdom, and unity. Their journey will determine the fate of the forest and transform them into heroes.

1. https://books2read.com/u/4Xlqna

2. https://books2read.com/u/4Xlqna

About the Author

Patrick William Lee is a renowned author celebrated for his enchanting tales of magic and wonder. Specializing in the genres of fairy tales, folk tales, legends, and mythology, Patrick weaves stories that transport readers to fantastical realms where the impossible becomes reality. With a deep love for folklore and a talent for crafting timeless narratives, his books captivate the imaginations of readers young and old. When he's not writing, Patrick enjoys exploring ancient forests, studying mythical creatures, and sharing his passion for storytelling with audiences around the world. His works continue to inspire and delight, leaving a lasting impact on the world of literature.

9 798227 504739